MY
LONE STAR
SUMMER

D. Anne Love

A Yearling Book

For Leanna Wilson Ellis,
fellow writer and beloved friend

Published by
Bantam Doubleday Dell Books for Young Readers
a division of
Bantam Doubleday Dell Publishing Group, Inc.
1540 Broadway
New York, New York 10036

Visit us on the Web! www.bdd.com

**Educators and librarians, visit the BDD Teacher's
Resource Center at www.bdd.com/teachers**

ISBN: 0-440-41375-3

Reprinted by arrangement with Holiday House, Inc.

Printed in the United States of America

June 1998

10 9 8 7 6 5 4 3 2 1

OPM

MY
LONE STAR
SUMMER

Chapter One

Coming down the passenger ramp at the airport in Austin, I spotted my grandmother standing just inside the double glass doors. In jeans, boots and a shirt the color of Texas bluebonnets, she was hard to miss. I shifted my backpack and pushed through the crush of summer travelers, past the framed advertisements for real estate brokers and car rental companies, down the gray-carpeted hall and into her arms.

"Jill, darlin'! I thought you'd never get here."

"Hi, Gran." Already I felt happiness seeping into my bones, warming me like sunshine after a long winter. Since my parents' divorce, Mom and I had lived in California, but Gran's ranch in Texas was still the most home I knew.

She released me and held me at arm's length. "I swear you've grown another two inches since last year. And look at you. Pretty as a picture."

She was half right. I was definitely taller. But pretty? No way. Not by a long shot. She indicated my red backpack. "Is this all your luggage?"

"Are you kidding? You know Mom, she makes me pack everything I own, just in case."

"As if we don't have stores in Texas. Well, let's go get the rest of it."

Over her shoulder, I searched the crowd milling in the terminal. "Where's B.J.? I thought she was coming with you."

Gran's face clouded. "I thought so, too, but when I went by to pick her up, the house was locked and nobody was home."

B.J. Reynolds had been my best friend my whole life. I couldn't imagine summer at Gran's without her. Gran and I started down the concourse toward the baggage claim. "I can't believe she didn't come," I said. "She promised! It's practically a tradition."

"I don't blame you for being disappointed, but I'm sure she had a good reason," Gran said. "You two are like peas in a pod. She wouldn't miss your homecoming unless it was really important. Ah. Here we are."

We stopped at the luggage carousel. A buzzer sounded, a red light winked on, and suitcases and boxes spewed out the top and down the chute. After a moment, my two blue suitcases tumbled out. Since Mom had insisted on tying bright yellow yarn to the handles, they were pretty hard to miss. I hauled them off the revolving carousel and Gran hoisted the biggest one. "Is this everything?"

"Yeah, this is it." I picked up the other one and followed Gran to the exit. The automatic doors opened with a swoosh, and the heat, heavy and oppressive, enveloped me. We headed for the parking lot, Gran chattering a mile a minute.

". . . new minister for the church, and he's absolutely charming, and wait till you see what Eb has done with that old storage shed. What that boy can do with a saw and hammer is nearly miraculous."

I struggled to keep up with her strides and her conversation, but the heat and the heavy suitcase slowed me down. I'd forgotten how scorching Texas is in the summer. Out on the runway, a line of planes waited to take off. Heat waves shimmered above the concrete, turning the planes to masses of colored, wavy lines. The asphalt on the parking lot felt mushy beneath my sneakers. The air was heavy with the smell of jet fuel.

Gran stopped talking and turned back to me. "Oh, I'm sorry, honey. I didn't mean to run off and leave you."

She waited till I caught up, then smiled down at me. "Wait till you see what I just bought. You won't believe it."

We passed another lane of parked cars and stopped behind a brand-new convertible. Gran set my suitcase down and fished in her purse for her keys. "Ta daa!"

With a flourish, she inserted a key into the trunk and popped it open. I stared at her and then at the car. "Is this *yours?*"

"Isn't she a beaut?" Gran stowed my suitcases in the trunk and slammed it shut. "I've wanted a convertible my whole life, and when I sold off those cattle last month, I figured what the hey. I'm not getting any younger." She ran her fingers over the shiny surface. "Like it?"

I cupped my hands to the window and peered in at the red leather seats and the wood-paneled dash. "It's gorgeous, Gran."

She laughed. "I haven't told your mother yet. I know what *she'll* say, but I knew you'd be pleased!"

She unlocked the doors and we got in. She turned the key, pressed a button, and the roof folded back. I blinked against the blinding sunlight.

Gran opened a little compartment between

our seats and took out a pair of sunglasses. "I brought you these. I hope they're okay."

I slipped them on and checked my reflection in the outside mirror. "Cool. Thanks, Gran."

"You're welcome." She started the engine and we rolled out of the parking lot and onto the highway. Away from the airport, the air seemed cooler, and I settled back in my seat, letting the wind blow through my hair. I watched the scenery sliding by. On either side of the highway, the woods were a tapestry of brilliant greens and deep gray shadows, the meadows a carpet of lighter green, spangled with the bright yellows and reds of wildflowers. Clumps of cattle grazed lazily in the sun; horses stood beneath gnarled trees, swishing their broomlike tails.

After a while I closed my eyes, only half listening to my grandmother's animated chatter. The rush of wind through the open car, the feel of the hot sun on my bare arms, the honeyed cadence of my grandmother's voice above the road noise lulled me to a near sleep.

Then the car slowed abruptly as my grand-mother braked and honked the horn, and I sat up, wide awake. "Crazy fool!" Gran yelled. A rusted-out van sped by us, its radio blaring.

"That's a good way to get yourself killed!" she said to the back of the speeding van. To me she said, "Did I wake you up?"

"I wasn't really asleep." I watched the high-way unfolding before us, thinking again about B.J. It wasn't like her to break a promise. I hoped she wasn't sick. I hoped I hadn't done anything to make her mad at me.

"So," Gran said, "how was school this year?"

"Okay, I guess. Right at the end I had to tutor some guy in English. Thanks to Addie Webb and her big mouth."

"Oh?" Gran glanced over at me. "And who is Addie Webb?"

"The smartest girl in our school. And she told Mrs. Riley I would tutor Jeff Thomas so he wouldn't fail the final test."

"I see. How come somebody else was speak-ing for you? Cat get your tongue?"

I could feel myself blush. Gran has this thing about being assertive. "I was daydreaming," I admitted. "About coming back here."

"Is that so?" She glanced in the mirror and cruised past an eighteen-wheeler as if it were standing still. "It's best to keep your mind on your studies, but since you were thinking about visiting your poor old grandma, I'll forgive you this time."

I pretended to wipe sweat off my brow. "Whew! What a relief."

"Don't be cute," she said. "School is important."

"School is boring."

She ignored that. "So tell me. Were you able to salvage that poor boy's English grade?"

"He got a B," I said.

"And what about you?"

"An A." I made the announcement as modestly as I could, but the truth is I was really proud of it. Mrs. Riley had a reputation as the toughest teacher in school. Her favorite saying was that A's didn't grow on trees.

Gran nodded her approval. "Good girl. I'll bet your mother was pleased."

"She barely noticed," I said, "on account of Robert."

We rolled up to a four-way stop and Gran looked over at me. "Who's Robert?"

"You mean she hasn't told you?"

Gran drove through the intersection. "You know how your mother is. If it weren't for your letters, I wouldn't know *anything* that goes on out there."

"It's this guy she met at work. They've been going out a lot lately."

"Is it serious?"

I shrugged. "It's hard to tell. You know Mom."

"What's he like?" Gran grinned conspiratorially. "Is he cute?"

Somehow it was hard to think of a forty-year-old man as cute.

"He's not bad, for an old guy, but he's totally clueless." My sunglasses had slipped down on my nose and I pushed them back into place.

"The first time he came to take Mom out, he brought me this really dorky present."

"Dorky?" Gran asked. Too late, I remembered how much she hated slang.

"Stupid," I amended. "He brought me a stupid present. A doll that wets and cries. Like I'm about four years old."

Gran slowed the car and signaled for a turn. We turned off the highway and onto the two-lane road that led to her ranch. I shifted impatiently in my seat. Even the memory of that mortifying present couldn't dull my excitement at being almost home.

"A doll, huh?" Gran picked up the thread of the conversation. "Maybe he was a little off base there, but give the poor man credit for trying. Chivalry may not be dead yet, but it's certainly mortally wounded. I remember when your grandfather came calling, he always—"

She broke off as a black pickup careered around us on the narrow road. The driver honked his horn, swerved back into our lane, then hit the brakes as he approached a sharp curve. The two people standing in the back swayed with the motion of the truck, yelling and shrieking with laughter. I looked up and a sickening knot coiled in the pit of my stomach. One of those howling idiots was a strange boy in cutoff jeans and sunglasses. The other one was B.J.

Chapter Two

I love the ranch. It's been in my family for three generations. My mom was born in the house where Gran still lives. I lived there until I was two. Then Mom and Dad built a house of their own closer to town. Even after we moved, I still loved Gran's place best, with its ancient trees, the shimmer of early morning light on the slow-moving river, the chirping of crickets and the frogs, the greenish-yellow glow of fireflies in the summer twilight. I still love listening to the night sounds, counting the stars, and thinking up new things to do with B.J.

When we were little, we made mud pies in the shade of Gran's pecan trees out back and chased frogs along the riverbank, but when we got to fourth grade, we got bikes for Christmas. After that, we rode all over the ranch, along the dirt road as far upriver as China Grove and past the dank-smelling caves down by the old Hallaby place.

Our favorite spot lies just beyond a bend in the river. There, the river runs so deep that you can't see the bottom unless you're lying on your stomach with your face practically in the water. Then you can see the shapes of smooth rocks lying half-buried in the mud, the lazy catfish feeding there, and the dark, turning shadows of the snakes that live along the banks. A huge elm tree split in two by lightning juts out across the dark water, and its branches form a natural bench that's just right for both of us. It's a perfect spot for best friends, and it's only big enough for two.

The morning after I got to the ranch, I put on a pair of denim shorts and a T-shirt, made a couple of sandwiches, stuffed a couple of cans of cola in my backpack, and rode out to the river. I couldn't wait to find out why B.J.

had spent yesterday afternoon in the back of a pickup with some boy instead of meeting me at the airport like she'd promised; why she hadn't answered her phone all night.

I put the cans in the water to keep them cool and climbed onto the smooth end of the elm tree to wait for her. High above me, a mockingbird chattered for a few minutes, then swept away through the trees. I took out my pen to write a note to Mom. Then I saw B.J. coming through the trees toward the river with the boy from the pickup. He wore black shorts and a white T-shirt, and his face was half hidden behind those dumb-looking wraparound sunglasses. Something must have been terribly funny, because they were laughing like two wild hyenas.

B.J. shaded her eyes with one hand and looked up at me. "Jill! Hi!" That was all. We hadn't seen each other in a year, but she was acting as if it had been only minutes instead of twelve whole months.

"Hi," I said. I couldn't believe she was so

dressed up. She wore hot-pink shorts with a matching shirt. Her blond hair, which is usually as straight and unruly as mine, curled around her shoulders as if she'd just come from the beauty shop. In place of her usual grubby tennis shoes, she wore new white sandals. Her lips and toenails were painted bright pink. In other words, she looked like a movie star. And I felt as ugly as the bark on the trees. But something else was bothering me. "How come you didn't show up at the airport yesterday? You promised to come with Gran to pick me up."

"That was my fault," the boy said quickly. "I asked her to go with Dad and me to buy lumber, and it took longer than we planned. I'm sorry I made her late."

I shot him a murderous look. I said to B.J., "Where were you last night? I called your house at least ten times, and nobody answered."

The boy raised his hand, as if he were answering a question in school. "My fault again. I invited her to have supper with us."

B.J. shook out her curls. "I wanted to call you when I got home last night, but Mom wouldn't let me. She said it was too late." She smiled at the boy. "Jill, this is Trey Wilborn. His family just bought the old Hallaby place."

"Hullo," the boy said from behind his dark glasses.

"Hi," I mumbled to the toe of my shoe. "What would anybody want that old place for?"

"They're tearing down the old farmhouse and building a brand-new one," B.J. explained. "They'll be moved in by the time school starts, and guess what? Trey's in ninth grade, so he'll go to the same school as me. Isn't that great?"

"Terrific." I slammed my notebook shut. "B.J., are you going to stand there yelling at me all day, or are you coming up here?"

"B.J.?" Trey cut in.

B.J. tossed her curly mane and smiled at Trey. "That was my nickname when I was a kid." She squinted up at me. "I prefer Belinda now, if you don't mind."

"Okay, *Belinda.* Are you coming up here or not?"

"In these clothes? They're brand new. My mom will kill me if I ruin them."

"Well then," I said. "I don't know why you even bothered to come down here if you're just going to stand there hollering at me."

"Why, to say hi and welcome home, Jill."

I could see that I had hurt her feelings, but she deserved it. She'd hurt mine by not showing up at the airport, then by bringing this strange boy to our secret place on the river, and by making me feel so incredibly ugly.

"Besides," she went on, "I wanted you to meet Trey. He's camping out with his family in an RV while they're building the house." She rested her hand on his arm. "I think it would be so cool to camp out all summer."

"Yeah," Trey said.

"Listen," B.J. said to me. "We're going to the Dairy Queen for a Coke. Trey's cousin is taking us in his truck. Want to come along?"

"No thanks. I have to help Gran."

"She'll let you go with us, Jill. Let's go ask her."

"She's not home," I said. "She's out checking on the cattle."

"Oh," B.J. said. "Later, then. Come on, Trey. We don't want Ricky to leave without us." She waved at me and turned back toward the road.

I watched them disappear into the trees and tried to swallow the lump in my throat. I hung around the river a while longer, watching the squirrels. I skipped a few rocks across the water. But without B.J., nothing was fun, and I took the soft drink cans out of the water and rode back to the house.

I found Gran in the peach orchard. I leaned my bike against the shady side of the porch, took an empty basket from the shed and went to help her. She looked down at me from the top step of the ladder, both her hands full of ripe peaches.

"Back so soon? Where's B.J.?"

"It's *Belinda* now," I said, "and she's gone to the Dairy Queen. With a boy."

"Oh?" Gran murmured. "Who?"

"Remember that boy riding in the back of the truck with her yesterday? Well, that's Trey Wilborn. His family bought the Hallaby place. B.J. said they're tearing it down to build a new one."

Gran nodded. "Seems I remember reading in the paper that that place had been sold, but I didn't realize they'd be moving in so soon." She dumped the peaches into her basket and wiped her face on the sleeve of her shirt. "We'll have to invite both of them to supper on Sunday."

"I don't want to invite *him*. Or B.J. either if she's going to act so stuck up. She's wearing lipstick, Gran, and toenail polish!"

The corners of Gran's mouth twitched into a tiny smile, but I didn't see anything the least bit funny about the way B.J. was acting.

"Don't be too hard on her, sweetie. There's nothing wrong with a girl's wanting to look her best. Here. Give me another basket."

I handed her an empty basket. "Why can't she just be herself?" I complained. "She wouldn't even come up in the tree because she didn't want to mess up her precious new clothes. Nobody wears new stuff in the summer, Gran."

Gran came down off the ladder and put her arm around me. "B.J.'s trying to grow up. Be patient with her."

"Why did she have to bring him down to the river anyway?" I persisted. "That's the best spot. Now we'll never have it to ourselves."

"Oh, I don't know about that," Gran said. "I imagine Trey's daddy's expecting some help building that house. That should keep him out of your hair for a while."

She handed me the baskets of peaches and folded the stepladder. "Let's go put these in the freezer."

Putting peaches in the freezer is a lot more complicated than it sounds. You can't just throw them in there. First you drop them in boiling water to loosen the skins, then dunk them in cold water to make them easier to peel. You take out the pits, slice them, and mix them with sugar and some powdered stuff called pectin. Then you put them into plastic bags, and finally they're ready for the freezer.

It's a messy job. By the time we finished, it was late afternoon and my fingers, my shirt, the kitchen counter—even the white porcelain sink—were stained an icky orange. Gran's cheeks were flushed from standing over the boiling water, and her dark curls lay plastered to her forehead.

"I don't know about you, but I'm too tired to cook," she said, wiping her face. "Let's go out for supper."

I helped her load the dishwasher and mop the floor, and then I took a long shower. I put on my nicest pair of shorts and the pink T-shirt I got at a concert in L.A. I borrowed Gran's hair dryer and fluffed my hair out around my shoulders. Then I stood in front of the mirror and bit my lips till they hurt, trying to look as pretty as B.J. It was no use. I looked too skinny, too brown, too plain. Mousy, if you want to know the honest truth.

"You look very nice," Gran said from the doorway.

I unplugged the hair dryer. "You're biased. I'm a mess."

"Nonsense." She dangled the car keys in front of me. "Want to drive the Mustang?"

"Sure!" I hugged her. She smelled great. Like summer lilacs. "I love you, Gran."

She laughed. "I love you, too. But if you tell your mother I let you drive, she'll have us both for cat food."

We went out to the little convertible and I sat as close to Gran as I could get. I watched her turn the ignition key and move the shift lever from Park to Reverse. Gran spun the car around, heading it down the gravel road toward the highway.

"Give me your hand." She showed me how to move the shift from Reverse to Drive. Then she let out on the brake and the car rolled down the hill.

I craned my neck and looked through the windshield. The leather steering wheel felt solid in my hands. A shiver crawled along my spine. I was driving!

It was so easy. At the slightest touch of the wheel, the car went exactly where I wanted it to.

"Watch it!" Gran said suddenly. "Pothole."

I jerked the wheel to the right and the car left the road and bounced along the edge of the pasture. Gran hit the brakes and a cloud of dust swirled up, hanging in the air like powdered gold. Gran's sweet-faced calf, Puddin, gazed calmly at us from the other side of the fence.

"Sweetie, are you hurt?"

"I'm okay," I said shakily. "Are you all right, Gran?"

"Perfectly fine." She brushed the dust from her sleeves, eased the car back onto the road and put my hands on the wheel again. "You turned too sharply back there, but it was my fault. I scared you."

I gripped the wheel and concentrated on the gravel road, but driving didn't seem fun anymore and I was relieved when we got to the highway and Gran took over.

"You did just fine," she said. "Next time, you'll do even better." She glanced into the rearview mirror and eased into the slow lane. "Before you know it, you'll have a license and a car of your own. Why, I can just imagine you zipping along the highways out West in a car like this, with a surfboard sticking out the back!"

I huddled in the red leather seat. "I guess."

She glanced over at me. "What's wrong? Still thinking about B.J.?"

Tears stung my eyes and my throat closed up like it does when I'm coming down with a cold. I nodded.

Gran pulled into the parking lot at the Texas Steakout. It was early, but the lot had already filled with pickup trucks and minivans and camping trailers with out-of-state license plates. Clouds of gray smoke billowed from the outdoor cooking pit. The air smelled of burning wood and barbecue sauce.

The green neon restaurant sign flashed off and on, reflecting off Gran's glasses. She turned to me. "Come on now, Jill. Don't be so glum. It'll all work out. By tomorrow, B.J.'ll be down at the river looking and acting like her old self."

"As long as she doesn't bring that Trey person with her."

Gran thought for a moment. "Suppose B.J. came to visit you. Wouldn't you introduce her to that little Japanese girl you met last year? What was her name?"

"Noriko."

"Wouldn't you introduce B.J. to Noriko?"

I shrugged. "I guess so."

It wasn't the same thing. Not at all. But I didn't feel like arguing with Gran.

"You see?" Gran's eyes reminded me of Mom's—serious and friendly at the same time. "You can't expect B.J. not to make other friends, Jill. After all, you live so far away, and you're both growing up. But that doesn't have to change things between you."

She reached across the seat and hugged me. "Come on, now. Cheer up. Let's go eat. I'm starved!"

I followed her into the restaurant and we sat in a booth at the back, right by the jukebox. A boy in tight jeans and a denim jacket put some quarters in, and the music spilled out so loud that it was impossible to talk, even if I'd felt like it.

Gran smiled at me and drummed her bright red fingernails on the side of her iced tea glass. I leaned against the cracked vinyl seat and waited for our steaks to come, wondering about B.J. and Trey. Were they still at the Dairy Queen with his cousin Ricky, or were they sitting in my elm tree down on the river, watching the sun slide down the sky and laughing their silly heads off?

Chapter Three

B.J. showed up the next morning while I was still having breakfast. Cupping her hands to her face, she peered through the screen door. "Hey, Jill. Can I come in?"

"Hi, honey!" Gran answered for me. "Come on in. We're having blueberry pancakes."

B.J. opened the door and let it slap shut. She pulled out the chair next to mine and smiled up at Gran. "I'll have just one, Mrs. Lawrence." She patted her perfectly flat stomach. "Have to watch my figure."

I stared at her, stunned at her preoccupation with her looks, remembering the summer in second grade when Mrs. Reynolds threatened to chop all of B.J.'s hair off because she wouldn't brush it. No danger of that now. Every hair was in place, making her seem way too perfect for somebody our age.

I glanced at the stack of half-eaten pancakes on my plate and then at my own middle. Batter sizzled on the griddle and Gran flipped the pancake over. B.J. waited, sipping daintily at a glass of water. Watching her graceful movements, I felt as fat and awkward as one of Gran's cows. I pushed my plate away and dumped the rest of my milk down the sink.

"Finished?" Gran smiled at me and set a plate in front of B.J.

"Yes ma'am." I put my plate in the dishwasher and sat down opposite B.J. She poured a generous teaspoon of syrup on her pancake, then cut it into tiny little pieces and nibbled on them with all the gusto of a rabbit eating lettuce.

Gran took off the blue-flowered apron she'd tied over her exercise clothes. "Excuse me, girls, I have an appointment with Jane Fonda."

"Huh?" B.J.'s brows went up.

"Gran's exercise tape," I explained. "Her aerobics teacher has the flu this week."

"Oh."

Gran went out to the living room and switched on the VCR.

B.J. downed one last bite of pancake and helped herself to another glass of water. "What do you want to do today?" she asked. She dabbed her mouth with her napkin.

"I dunno. We could go fishing."

"I don't think so. It's starting to rain."

I looked out. Raindrops trickled down the windows, making wavy lines on the dusty panes. "Let's go to my room," I said, and we went down the hall and closed the door. I took a game board from the shelf. "How about Monopoly?"

"Naw," B.J. said. "You always win."

I stood on tiptoe and peered into the closet. "Scrabble?"

"That word game?" She shook her head. "It's too much like Mrs. Patterson's English class. Remember how she made us do twenty-five vocabulary words every Monday?"

"Okay," I said. "I give up. What do *you* want to do?"

She pulled a cassette tape from her pocket. "We could listen to this. I got it yesterday at the mall."

I looked at the picture of the six long-haired singers dressed in black leather pants and miles of silver chains. "Does your mom know you bought this?"

B.J. grinned. "Are you kidding? She'd have a cow. She's not modern, like your gran."

"I don't think even Gran would like this," I said. But I took out my cassette player and B.J. slid the tape in. We lay on the bed, listening. All the songs sounded pretty much the same to me, but B.J. seemed positively transported. She closed her eyes and played air guitar, her head bobbing in time to the music.

Between songs, we caught up on a year's worth of news. I told her about the report I'd written on tree frogs for science class, and how Mr. Stein had said it was the best one he'd ever read.

B.J. wrinkled her nose. "Tree frogs? Yuck.

Why didn't you pick something cute, like koalas, or deer? Fawns are so darling!"

"I didn't want to write about something *darling*. I wanted to write about something interesting. Did you know that tree frogs change colors when the temperature changes?"

"Fascinating," B.J. said, in a tone that plainly said she was unimpressed. "Forget about frogs. I've got big news." She sat up on the bed and folded her legs under her, Indian style. "Guess what?"

"What?" I turned the music down. From the living room came the sound of Gran's feet shuffling and thumping on the carpet.

"Remember Miss Jensen in fourth grade?"

"How could I forget her?" I asked. "She was the greatest teacher ever."

"She's not coming back next year," B.J. said. "She's going to have a baby."

"Miss *Jensen?* You're kidding!"

"I'm totally serious! She's Mrs. Whiting now. The teachers had a shower for her and everything. Even her husband came." B.J.

closed her eyes and sighed. "I swear, Jill, he is so gorgeous he makes my teeth ache." She smiled dreamily. "Just think, a handsome husband and a new baby. It's so romantic, I could just die."

"Aunt Gina had a baby last fall," I said. "All he does is eat, sleep and cry. And he leaks at both ends."

B.J. hooted. "There's not a romantic bone in your body, Jill."

In the next room, we could hear Jane Fonda cheering Gran on. *"Come on, now, get it up,"* Jane said. *"Just think, you're almost through with the whole class."*

B.J. rolled off the bed, stretched out on the floor and started raising first one leg and then the other in the air.

"What on earth are you doing?" I asked.

"Leg lifts. So I won't get fat."

"You're impossible." I got up and punched the Stop button on the tape player.

"Want to know a secret?" B.J. asked from her place on the floor. Her legs went up and down, up and down.

"What?" I lifted the curtain and looked out. The rain fell harder, obscuring the barn and the orchards beyond.

"Promise you won't tell. Scout's honor."

B.J. got off the floor and stood in front of me. "Look."

She lifted her mass of blond hair. A tiny gold bead shone in each of her ear lobes. She grinned. "Pierced ears! Melissa Mason did it for me at her house Wednesday night. Cool, huh?"

"Sounds painful," I said. "How did she do it?"

"With a needle and ice cubes. She numbed my ears with the ice and stuck the needle through." B.J. made a jabbing motion in the air. It made my ears throb just to think about it.

"It didn't hurt at all," B.J. declared. "And she put these little posts in the holes. Real gold."

Gran stuck her head into the room. She had finished her tape. Her hair was still damp from her shower, and she'd changed into jeans and a yellow cotton shirt. "Rain's letting up. I'm going to take the pickup over to the barn and see how Eb is doing with the new calves."

Eb helps Gran run the ranch. He feeds the cattle, shoes the horses, fixes the fences. He's kind of quiet, but he always smiles and tips his beat-up Stetson when he sees me out with Gran.

"There's plenty of sandwich meat in the fridge," Gran went on. She turned to B.J. "Can you come for supper tonight? If this rain stops, we'll make hamburgers on the grill."

"Great!" B.J. grinned at Gran. "I'll ask Mom, but I'm sure it's okay."

Gran shot me her I-told-you-so look and closed the door behind her. We listened to the hollow tread of her boots along the wooden porch and then the sputtering of the pickup engine.

B.J. flopped down on the bed. "What do you wanna do now?"

I shrugged. She'd already nixed all my suggestions. Outside, rain dripped from the leaves of the trees and plinked into the metal tub beneath the eaves of the house. The hall clock chimed eleven. Thunder echoed across the hills. I switched on the pink ballerina lamp that had been my mother's. "You wanna read? I brought some new mysteries."

"Naw." B.J. sat up and eyed me for a long time. Then she said, "I know! We can pierce your ears!"

I stared at her. "You're crazy!"

"Why not?" She pulled my hair away from my face and stood at arm's length, considering. "You'd be really cute with pierced ears, Jill, and it wouldn't be hard to do at all."

I twisted away from her. "You are not sticking a needle through my ears!"

"Why not?" she said again.

"Because it's stupid!"

"It is not stupid. Practically everybody at my school has already done it. Even some of the second-graders."

"Well, some of the kids at my school wear

rings in their noses and dye their hair purple, but that doesn't mean I have to."

B.J.'s eyes glittered like the sapphires in Gran's wedding ring. "Scaredy cat!"

"I'm not scared," I said. "I just don't see any reason to punch holes in my ears."

B.J. folded her arms across her chest. "Come on, Jill," she coaxed. "It won't hurt half as bad as that bee sting you got last summer down at the river. I promise." She gave me her most convincing smile. "We could go shopping in Austin and get matching pairs of earrings. We could be twins! Wouldn't that be cool?"

Well, that did it. The night before, at the restaurant with Gran, I could hardly eat for worrying that I was losing my best friend. If having my ears pierced would save our friendship, it would be worth it, no matter what. I looked at B.J. for a minute. "You promise it won't hurt?"

"Hardly at all!" She beamed at me. "This will be so neat, Jill. We can exchange earrings through the mail and everything."

She took another look at my ears. "Where's your Gran's sewing kit?"

"I'll get it." I went down the hall to the sewing room and took Gran's wicker basket off the shelf. Ice rattled in the kitchen. B.J. stuck her head through the door of the sewing room.

"Got any alcohol?"

"What for?"

"To sterilize the needle."

"Oh." I ignored the sickening lurch in my stomach. "In the bathroom."

I opened the basket and took out Gran's apple-shaped pincushion. Pins and needles glittered in the light. Just thinking about sticking those things in my ears made me dizzy. I took a deep breath and went back to my room.

B.J. sat me down at the dressing table and brushed my hair into a ponytail. Then she squatted in front of me until her face was even with mine and made a dot with an ink pen on my ear lobes. She handed me two ice cubes wrapped in paper towels. "Here. Hold these against your ears while I get the needle ready."

After a few minutes, the paper towels turned soggy and the melting ice dribbled down my arms and off my elbows. But my ears did feel numb, and I relaxed a little. Maybe it wouldn't hurt after all.

B.J. dipped a needle into the bottle of alcohol. "Be still now," she instructed and before I knew what was happening, she jabbed the needle through my ear lobe.

"*Ow!*" Tears sprang to my eyes. I jumped out of the chair. "You've killed me!"

"Good grief!" B.J. said. "I have not killed you. Sit down. I have to do the other one."

"In your dreams! It *hurts*, B.J."

She sighed. "Okay then, crybaby. Forget it." She put the cap on the alcohol bottle and tossed the needle onto the dresser.

I held the soggy paper towels to my ear, waiting for the pain to stop.

"I gotta go," she said. She sounded disgusted.

I looked up at her. Part of me loved her and part of me hated her, but I didn't want to go through the whole summer without her. Even if we couldn't wear matching earrings. "Are you still coming for supper tonight?"

She shrugged. "I guess so."

I let out a long breath. "Okay. See you then."

I followed her to the door. The rain had stopped. Shafts of sunlight slanted through the slate-colored clouds. Beneath their cloak of raindrops, Gran's pink azalea bushes sparkled in the light. Down at the end of the road, Eb's black truck sat next to Gran's red one.

B.J. hopped on her bike. "See ya."

I waved.

She disappeared through the stand of trees at the bend in the road. I tossed the soggy paper towels into the wastebasket and took my notebook into Granddad's library. After a while, Gran came back. She left her muddy boots on the front porch and padded through the house in her bright yellow socks, whistling a Willie Nelson tune. We made sandwiches and lemonade and ate on the back porch. After lunch, Gran took a nap and I read one of Mom's tattered Nancy Drew mysteries, and then we got ready to fix supper.

While Gran lit the grill, I shaped the hamburger patties and sliced the tomatoes. Gran made iced tea and cut a watermelon. When B.J. arrived, we cooked the burgers and watched a movie on TV. Eb came by with some chocolate ice cream and we ate it all, right from the carton.

Then Gran and I drove B.J. home in the convertible. The rain-washed night air felt cool on my face. Everything smelled new. I leaned my head back and watched the stars come out. In L.A., the city lights are so bright you can't see the stars; but here in Texas, they seem close enough to touch.

We dropped B.J. off and started home. Gran hummed a little tune and shook her hair out of her eyes. "Just look at that moon."

The clouds had cleared, and the full moon hung like a silver dollar in the sky. I smiled into the darkness.

"What did you two do today?" Gran asked.

I started to tell her about my one pierced ear, but I was too ashamed. I couldn't imagine Gran or Mom ever doing something so stupid. So I told Gran about listening to B.J.'s tape and about Miss Jensen's baby.

I put my finger to my ear. It throbbed and felt hot and sore. When we got home, I took some aspirin and went to bed, hoping it would feel better in the morning.

Chapter Four

I awoke with a start. It was still dark, but a pale moon cast a silvery light across my bed. I sat up. The whole side of my face felt hot and tingly, like a bad sunburn. I got out of bed, tiptoed across the hall to the bathroom and switched on the light.

My ear was the color of ripe tomatoes and so sore I couldn't stand to touch it. I pawed through the medicine cabinet, looking for something, anything, to make the hurting stop.

"Jill, honey, what's wrong?" Gran's voice made me jump. I turned around, tears already starting behind my eyes. Wordlessly, I pushed my hair away from my face.

"Oh, my heavens! How did this happen?"

She sat me down on the toilet seat and inspected my ear.

I told her what B.J. and I had done. "It hurt too much, Gran," I finished, "so I didn't let her do the other one."

"Well, thank goodness for that!" Gran's mouth tightened. "You've got a bad infection, young lady. Go put some clothes on."

"Where are we going?"

"To the emergency room. I don't think we should let this go till morning." She went back to her room without another word. I could tell she was mad at me for being so stupid. I wondered if she would send me home on the next plane, but my ear hurt so much I really didn't care.

I got dressed and waited for Gran in the living room. She came out in a pink warmup suit, her handbag over one arm, her keys in her hand. She hadn't stopped to put on makeup, and for the first time I noticed the fine lines around her eyes and mouth. In the dim glow of the lamplight, she looked old and tired, and

I felt ashamed for having caused her so much trouble.

"I'm sorry, Gran," I said. "I didn't mean to make such a mess of things."

"I know you didn't. Hurry up now. Let's go."

She hardly spoke on the trip to the hospital. When we got to the emergency room entrance, she pulled into a parking space right by the door and led me through the sliding glass doors to the desk. The night nurse looked up from her magazine. "What happened?"

"Do-it-yourself cosmetology," Gran explained. "I think her ear is infected."

The nurse sighed and rolled her eyes. "This is the third one this week," she said to Gran. "You'd think those girls would know better." She looked down at me. "Both ears?"

"No, just the right," I mumbled.

"Come on, then." She led me to a room with blue walls and a white floor, helped me onto a table and covered my feet with a blanket. "Doctor will be here in a minute," she said. "I'll be right back."

I didn't want to stay there alone, but I was too embarrassed to say so, and too afraid to ask for Gran after all the trouble I'd caused. I closed my eyes against the blinding overhead lights and thought about the beach in California, Mrs. Riley's English class, anything to take my mind off my throbbing ear.

Finally footsteps squeaked on the tile floor and a man in a green coat bent over me. "I hear you've got a bad ear," he said.

I nodded.

"Let's take a look." He smoothed my hair back, peered at my ear and whistled softly. "What did you use, a rusty nail?"

"A sewing needle."

He shook his head. "Next time you decide your body requires additional orifices, let a doctor do it."

He opened a bottle of strong-smelling liquid and dabbed at my ear with a cotton swab. Right away the pain stopped. I could have kissed him.

I heard a rustling sound and Gran appeared at my bedside, her hands full of papers. She looked at the doctor. "How bad is it?"

"I've seen worse," he said. "An injection and a few days of antibiotics should do the trick."

Before I knew what was happening, I felt the prick and sting of a needle in my arm.

"There now." He smiled down at me. "By tomorrow, you should feel a lot better."

"Thanks," I said.

"Okay." He washed his hands at the sink and handed Gran a tube of medicine. "Put this on her ear twice a day, and call your family doctor if you don't see a big improvement in a couple of days." He grinned at me. "Stay away from sewing needles, young lady."

"I will." I watched him disappear down the hall. Gran dropped the medicine into her purse and helped me off the table. We went back to the nurse's desk and Gran gave her the papers. Then we went outside.

It was nearly morning. The air was still cool; the sky, the color of liquid pearls. I got in the car and rested my head against the seat. Gran backed out of the parking lot, and we drove through the deserted city streets toward the highway and home.

After a long time, Gran said, "Feeling better?"

"Yes ma'am," I said. "Gran, I'm sorry. I was afraid B.J. wouldn't be friends with me unless I pierced my ears. And anyway, Melissa Mason did B.J.'s ears and nothing happened."

"B.J. was lucky," Gran said. "And let me tell you something. A real friend won't force you to do something you don't feel is right."

She didn't have to tell me that. There's a lot in life I haven't figured out yet, but that much I knew.

I studied her face, bathed in the green glow of the dashboard lights, thankful she was still speaking to me after the stupid stunt I'd pulled. "I love you, Gran," I said.

"I love you, too, pumpkin." She leaned across and kissed my temple. I slept the rest of the way home.

*   *   *

A pair of dirty sneakers dangled above the river. I looked up in our tree, and B.J. grinned down at me. "I thought you'd never get here."

I scrambled up and settled down beside her. The branches rustled and swayed beneath my weight. "Gran made me take a nap. She's still worried about my ear."

"Gosh, I'm really sorry, Jill." B.J.'s eyes looked like blue saucers. "I never dreamed you'd get sick."

"Me either. But I'll live."

"Is your Gran still mad?" She handed me a soft drink.

I popped the top and took a long sip. "I think she's mostly over it, but I'm trying to stay out of her way for a while."

B.J. nodded. "That's what I figured." She leaned back and closed her eyes, stretching like a cat just waking from a nap. "Guess who I saw this morning?"

"Who?" I closed my eyes, too, letting the sun warm my face.

"Trey. He was up on the roof, no shirt on, wearing this really dorky hat, helping his dad put on shingles. He looked so adorable, I could have squeezed him to pieces."

"Hmm."

"Don't you think he's totally cool, Jill?"

I opened my eyes. B.J. stared dreamily into the distance. I shrugged. "He doesn't talk much."

"That's because he's real shy at first," B.J. said. "After you get to know him, he talks about lots of things."

"Like what?" I took another sip of cola, but it had turned lukewarm. I poured the rest of it into the river and flattened the can.

"Oh, music. And astronomy. He knows everything there is to know about that. He has his own telescope and everything. He promised to show me how to use it after his house is done."

A wave of loneliness washed over me. By then I would be back in California and B.J. would be here, palling around with Trey. I don't know why that bothered me so much, but it did. I changed the subject.

"Who'd you get for math next year?"

B.J. made a face. "Mr. Hooper. The terror of North Junior High. But I got Mrs. Gresham for science, and guess what? She's going to be the cheerleader sponsor, too." Her expression grew serious. "Gosh, I hope I make the squad, Jill. If I don't I'll just die."

She inched her way out to the end of the tree branch and dropped lightly to the riverbank. "I've been practicing," she called up to me. "Watch!"

She raised both hands over her head in a perfect V. "Give me a V!" she yelled, spinning around on one foot. "Give me an I!" She leaped high into the air and kicked out with one leg. "Give me a C-T-O-R-Y!" She turned a perfect cartwheel and landed in a split on the grass, both hands over her head. "Victory, victory, victory, yeah!"

She squinted up at me. "How was it? Did I keep my legs straight?"

"That was really great," I said. I couldn't turn a cartwheel if my life depended on it.

B.J. jumped up and scrambled back up beside me, her skin pink, her ponytail falling down. Tiny beads of sweat stood on her forehead, and she still looked beautiful. I had no doubt she'd make the squad.

"Sue Ellen Coates is helping me with my routine," B.J. said. "She's going to be head cheerleader at the high school next year."

I nodded, remembering when Sue Ellen stayed with B.J. and me when our parents went out for the evening. I could still remember her megawatt smile and her dark ponytail bouncing up and down as she practiced her cheers on our front lawn.

"You should go out for cheerleader at your school," B.J. urged. "It's a lot of fun."

I shook my head. "I'd break my neck. Besides, I'm on the newspaper staff next year, and Mom only allows one activity at a time. She worries about my grades."

"What for?" B.J. said. "You're a real brain. *I'm* the one who should worry."

"You just don't apply yourself, Belinda," I said, in the voice Miss Jensen used in fourth grade when she handed B.J.'s papers back.

B.J. giggled. "That's perfect, Jill. You should be a teacher."

"Not me. I'm going to be a reporter."

"Well then," B.J. said. "I've got a news flash for you. Check this out." She skinned her T-shirt over her head. "Well? What do you think?"

I stared at the two little triangles of lace and elastic covering her chest. "How come you're wearing that thing? It looks like a harness!"

Her face clouded. "Because my mom thought it was time," she said. "In case you haven't noticed, Jill, I'm not a little kid anymore."

She pulled her shirt back on and picked up her empty cola can. "I gotta go."

I followed her to the ground. "B.J., don't go running off. I didn't mean to hurt your feelings. I was just surprised, that's all."

"Forget it." She got on her bike. "I'm meeting Sue Ellen at her house. We're practicing my routine. See ya."

I jumped on my bike and pedaled as fast as I could in the opposite direction. What was happening to us? It seemed that every time we were together, one of us ended up wounded.

I was still thinking about it two days later when I got back to the river. B.J. wasn't there, so I watched the squirrels and mockingbirds scolding and chattering in the trees. I tossed a few leaves into the sun-brightened water and watched them swirl downstream, thinking about what Gran had said about how B.J. was trying to grow up, and how I should be patient with her. Well, B.J. and I are both twelve, but you don't see me trying to act like a grown woman and getting so touchy every time somebody says something to me.

I heard a familiar rustling in the grass and felt a grin spread across my face. "Hey!" I yelled. "B.J.! Up here!"

"Hey!" said a strange voice.

I looked down. It was Trey.

Chapter Five

For once he wasn't wearing those ridiculous sunglasses. He shaded his eyes with one hand and said, "Can I come up?"

I still felt protective of our tree, even if B.J. and I weren't having much fun in it this year. So I said, "I was just coming down!" and I slid out to the edge and dropped to the ground. When I straightened up, I saw that his eyes were dark, like mine, and his nose was sprinkled with golden freckles. On him they looked nice, though, and I smiled at him. I couldn't help it.

"Hey," he said.

"Hi." I dusted off the seat of my shorts and raked my fingers through my hair. "B.J.'s not here."

"I know. She went to Dallas with her mother."

I shook my head. "She wouldn't leave without telling me."

He shrugged. "Want to hang out for a while?"

"I thought you had to help your dad on the house."

"We ran out of shingles and can't get more till day after tomorrow." He grinned. "Till then, I'm a free man."

"We could ride up to China Grove," I offered, "or down to the caves."

"I don't have a bike," Trey said. "It's still at our house in Santa Fe."

"Oh. What do you want to do, then?"

"Can you skateboard?"

"I never learned." I wasn't about to tell him I was the world's klutziest human—and a coward besides.

"It's not exactly rocket science," Trey said. "Come on. I'll show you."

I chained my bike to a tree and followed

him along the riverbank and across the pasture to the Hallaby place.

If it hadn't been for the gnarled oak trees still standing in the front yard, I'd never have recognized it. The old house was gone and in its place rose the beginnings of a new one. It had no windows or doors yet, but most of the roof was on. In front a new concrete driveway gleamed, white as bleached bones. To one side, beneath the sheltering trees, sat the silver-and-blue RV that B.J. had told me about.

Trey went inside and came back with a skateboard. "This," he said, holding it out to me, "is a skateboard."

"You're kidding," I said, and he grinned. He stood on the board and showed me how to push off with one foot, turn and stop.

"Now you try," he said.

I stood on the board and pushed off, and the board flew from under me. I sprawled on the concrete driveway. Trey retrieved the board and helped me back on it again. This time he held my hand, and I made it to the end of the driveway and back. After a while it got easier, like learning to ride a bike. Pretty soon I could skate, stop and turn without falling.

"This is really fun!" I said.

"Yeah. Watch this." Trey set the skateboard in motion, then ran to it, jumped on and flipped it into the air. He executed a perfect doughnut and brought the board to a stop right in front of me. "Your turn."

I should have known better, but I felt pretty confident after everything I'd already learned. Plus, I wanted to impress him. So I sent the skateboard rolling down the driveway, jumped on it and twisted around the way he had. The board flipped and my knee hit the sharp edge of the concrete. Blood spurted onto the ground.

I grabbed my knee and inspected the jagged cut, taking quick, deep breaths. I didn't want Trey to think I was a crybaby, but it hurt. Bad.

"Jeez, Jill, I'm sorry!" Trey pulled me to my feet and led me to the RV. He sat me down on the sofa and I heard doors opening and closing in the next room. In a minute he was back with a first aid kit. He soaked some cotton balls in alcohol and said, "This might sting a little."

He wasn't kidding. It hurt worse than my infected ear, but I clenched my teeth and watched him clean the dirt and blood. He opened the bandage packet and covered my knee with the patch. "There. That should do it."

"Thanks," I said.

"It was my fault. I shouldn't have been showing off." He wrapped the used cotton balls in a paper towel and threw them in the trash. "Want a Coke?"

"Okay."

I settled back on the sofa and looked around while Trey went to the refrigerator. I'd never been in an RV before. It was just like a miniature house. It had a living room with two little sofas and a table, and a tiny kitchen with a stove and sink. Two steps led up to another door. I figured the bedrooms were back there.

"How many people live here?" I asked.

Trey flopped down on the sofa opposite me and brushed his hair out of his eyes. "Just my folks and me, but it still gets pretty crowded when we're all here at once."

"How come you're moving here from Santa Fe?" I sipped the icy cola.

"My dad got a job teaching at the University of Texas."

"Oh yeah? What subject?"

His dark eyes narrowed. "What is this, Twenty Questions?"

I felt my face redden and I dropped my gaze. Mom always said I'd be perfect as a reporter because I've got more natural curiosity than a cat. But right then I wished the floor would open up and swallow me. "I—I'm sorry," I stammered. "I shouldn't be so nosy."

He smiled crookedly. "Forget it. For your information, Dad teaches astronomy."

When I didn't say anything, he said, "Astronomy's my hobby. What's yours?"

I shrugged. "I don't really have one, unless you count reading."

"You'd like astronomy," he said thoughtfully. "There are lots of unanswered questions in the stars."

I stared at him. He sounded so wise that it was hard to believe he was only a year or so older than I. He jumped up, wiping his hands on the sides of his cutoffs. "Wait here."

He went into the next room and came back with a telescope. "I got this for Christmas last year. When we get the house built, I'll have a special platform for it out back."

I ran my hands over the smooth metal cylinder and peered through the thick lens, racking my brain for an intelligent comment. Everything I knew about telescopes would have fit nicely on the head of a pin. "It's nice," I said lamely.

"One of the best made today. Dad got it in Germany." He opened a cabinet door and took out a thick book. "This tells about all the planets, constellations, everything."

I paged through the book, looking at the charts with numbers and lines and symbols that looked like little stars and moons.

"These are star maps," he explained. "With these, you can find any known star in the constellations." He pointed to a spot on one chart. "That's Sirius, the brightest known star. It's nine light-years away."

I frowned, wishing I'd paid more attention to Mr. Stein's science lessons last year. I wasn't sure how far a light-year was, but I knew it was really far.

Trey turned the page. "Here's the constellation Orion. Here's Carina, and Canis Major. That's where Sirius is located."

I watched and listened while he talked about Mars and Mercury and the phases of the moon. It was easy to see why he was so interested in astronomy. The sky was like a giant puzzle and the stars and moons and planets were pieces to be fitted into it. Listening to him, I realized B.J. was right. Once you got Trey to talking, he didn't have any trouble holding up his end of a conversation.

Then his dad pulled up outside and honked the horn. We went out and Trey introduced us. We said hi through the open windows of the truck and Trey climbed into the cab.

"Can we give you a lift?" Mr. Wilborn asked.

"No, thanks. I left my bike down by the river."

"Okay." Mr. Wilborn gave me a friendly smile. "Sorry to run off, but we have errands in Austin."

"That's okay," I said. "I should be getting home anyway."

Trey stuck his head out the window. "I had fun, Jill. Sorry about your knee."

"I'm okay," I said. "I had a good time, too."

Mr. Wilborn shifted the truck into reverse. "Bye now."

"Bye!" I waved till they turned the curve at the end of the road. Then I cut back across the pasture and got my bike. On the way home I couldn't stop thinking about how different Trey was from most boys I knew. He wasn't cruel and loud like Bruce Swearingen or dumb like Stanley Voss. He didn't act too old for his age, like some of the guys I knew. He definitely *was* what Gran would call "mannerly." I decided two things. One, I needed to read more about astronomy and two, we had to invite Trey to supper sometime soon.

When I got to the house, I found Gran sitting in the shade on the back porch, snapping beans. "There you are!" She got up and gave me a peck on the cheek. "I was about ready to send Eb out to—oh my gracious! What happened to your knee?"

"It's no big deal. Trey was teaching me to skateboard and—"

"Trey, huh?" Her dark eyes twinkled. "Does this mean you've called a truce?"

"He's nice, Gran. And anyway, B.J. never showed up."

"She's in Dallas with her folks. And you would know that if you'd bothered to check with me before you went flying out of here this morning. They'll be back Thursday." The screen door squeaked when Gran opened it. "You want some lunch?"

"I can fix it." We went in and I kicked my sneakers off and padded around barefoot on the cool tile floor. I made a peanut butter and banana sandwich and a glass of lemonade and took a couple of brownies from Gran's Tupperware bin. "Want a sandwich, Gran?"

"No thanks, dear. You go ahead. I think I'll finish these beans and run into town for a while. I need a few things at the store. You want to come?"

"No thanks." I bit into my sandwich.

"Suit yourself." Gran went back out to the porch. I finished my sandwich and went to Granddad's library to see if I could find a book about astronomy.

Chapter Six

When Granddad was alive, we had three hundred head of cattle on the ranch and eight or nine horses and a pond teeming with ducks. Back then, I'd snitch a loaf of bread from Gran's kitchen and sneak off to the pond to feed them. After a while they got to know me, and they'd start quacking like crazy when they saw me coming down the path with the Wonder bread bag tucked under my arm.

After Granddad died, Gran sold off most of the cattle and all but two of the horses, the pond filled up with silt and the ducks disappeared. Now Eb takes care of about fifty of Granddad's prize Hereford cattle. They're the same sturdy brown-and-white cattle President

Johnson raised on his ranch over in Stone-wall.

Most of the time Eb tools around the ranch in his battered pickup truck, but every once in a while he rides one of the horses. Gran named them Rhett and Scarlett, after her favorite characters in *Gone With the Wind*.

The morning after Trey taught me how to skateboard, I was sitting in the kitchen smearing Gran's strawberry jam on toast when Eb ambled in, tossed his beat-up Stetson on a chair and poured himself a cup of coffee. He nodded to me. "Mornin', Miss Jill."

"Morumpff," I said.

"Don't talk with your mouth full." Gran brought her cup to the table and sat down across from me. She looked up at Eb, lounging against the kitchen counter. "Well, Eb. What brings you here this time of the morning?" Her spoon made a little tinkling sound when she stirred her coffee.

He hooked his thumbs in his belt loops and grinned lazily. "Don't take long to feed fifty head o' cattle, ma'am." He winked at me. "When I was your age, my daddy ran a thousand head on our place in Montana. Worked that herd sunup to sundown, seven days a week."

I looked at him with new respect. I couldn't ever imagine riding herd on a thousand stubborn cows, but he talked as if it were the easiest thing in the world. Now he said to Gran, "I rode Rhett out this morning over by the old duck pond. You ever think about dredging that pond out, Miz Lawrence? It'd make a fine place for some ducks, come next spring."

Gran sighed and toyed with her spoon. "Oh, I don't know, Eb. It seems there's always something that needs fixing around here."

He nodded. "That's a fact. But you ought to see the meadow now that the grasses have come back. It's looking right pretty these days. Too bad Judge Lawrence isn't alive to appreciate it."

He blew on his coffee to cool it and took a long sip, watching my grandmother over the rim of his cup. "At least ride over with me and take a look at it. Old Scarlett could use the exercise."

Gran raised both her hands, palms out. "I give up! I might as well humor you right now and get it over with. But I can't waste all morning out there." She nodded toward a basket on the counter. "Those peaches have to go into the freezer today."

Eb grinned. "Won't be gone more'n an hour, I promise." He looked at me. "Why don't you come, too, kiddo? Your grandmother can make room for you in her saddle."

Gran took my hand. "Why *don't* you come along? I'll bet it's been years since you've been down to the pond."

"Okay." I gulped the last of my milk. "Can I saddle up Scarlett?"

"Are you sure you remember how?" Gran took our dishes to the sink and ran water over them.

"Yes ma'am." I slid my feet into my sneakers and went out to the pasture. The early morning air hinted at rain, and the dew-laden grass whispered beneath my feet.

Scarlett stuck her head over the fence, welcoming me with her chocolate-colored eyes.

"Hey, old girl." I stroked the white star on her forehead. She felt warm and soft as velvet and she smelled like hay and manure.

I led her out the gate and into the barn and put the saddle on her. Gran came out in boots and jeans and a bright red shirt. She handed me a straw hat that matched hers.

"Aw, Gran, I don't want to wear that thing. It's too hot."

Gran walked around Scarlett and checked to be sure I'd cinched the saddle. "It's better to be a little warm than to ruin your skin in this sun," she said. "When you're thirty, you'll thank your lucky stars I made you wear it. Come on, now, I haven't got all day."

She led Scarlett out of the barn, swung into the saddle as easily as if she were my age and held her hand out to me. I stuck my foot in the stirrup and settled into the saddle in front of her. Gran nudged the horse and picked up the reins.

We met Eb at the pasture and headed for the row of pecan trees bordering the river. Eb rode in front and Gran and I tagged along behind letting Scarlett take her time. When we reached the shade of the trees, we could hear the river tumbling over its rocky bed, and Gran hummed a little tune under her breath.

"What's that song?" I asked.

She chuckled softly. "Oh, gracious, Jill, I can't remember. Your grandfather used to sing it to me when we were courting."

"It's pretty." I pulled a leaf off a tree as we passed and stuck it behind my ear.

"I always thought so. Your granddad had a wonderful voice."

"I remember," I said. "He used to sing me to sleep every night."

"Remember this?" Gran started to sing: "Hush, little baby, don't say a word . . ."

"Papa's gonna buy you a mockingbird," I finished. "I never could figure out why you'd have to buy one, though. You could get a hundred of them around here for free."

Gran laughed and kissed the back of my neck. "You're too practical for your own good, my dear."

We rode out of the trees, then up a hill and down again into the meadow. Eb turned in his saddle and pointed across the stretch of spearmint-colored grass that seemed to go on forever. "Just over that rise is where the pond is. Or was."

"Oh, Eb." Something in Gran's voice made me turn around. She had taken off her sunglasses and I could see tears standing in her eyes. "The meadow really has come back."

"Yes ma'am," Eb said. "That fire pretty near done her in, but Mother Nature's a tough old bird." He swept his hand in the air. "This spot's prettier now than it ever was, if you ask me."

Sitting there in the saddle with Gran, I remembered times years ago when Granddad was still alive, before Mom and Dad got their divorce. We'd all come down to the meadow for a picnic of Gran's fried chicken and pecan pie. Sometimes we'd spend all afternoon and not go home till it was nearly dark. Then the fireflies would come out like tiny lanterns to guide us home.

Gran cleared her throat. "Well. Let's go take a look at that pond. That's what we came for."

Eb kicked Rhett into a smooth canter, and we followed on Scarlett—across the sea of grass and up to the edge of the pond.

We left the horses to graze and stood looking at what was left of the pond. Gran said, "It's hard to believe it ever held water."

"It's been five years, Miz Lawrence," Eb said. "But I reckon it wouldn't take long to put her to rights." He gestured toward the far side of the pond. "Take that spot over there, for instance. I figure that would be just about perfect for a little picnic table, couple of chairs, maybe. Be nice to sit out here of a summer's evening and listen to the frogs and birds."

"That *would* be nice, Gran," I said. "Maybe

we could get some ducks again. Like when I
was little."

Gran chuckled. "You and your ducks. I
couldn't believe you had names for all of
them."

"Me either," Eb said. "They all looked the
same to me."

"That's because you didn't get to know
them," I said. "They have different personali-
ties, just like people."

"I'll take your word for that, Miss Jill." Eb
turned to Gran. "I talked to the excavating
company over in Austin last week. Man there
said it wouldn't take more'n a couple days to
dig this all out again."

Gran sighed. "How much?"

"Seventy-five dollars an hour for two men
and the equipment."

"That's—"

"Twelve hundred dollars," I said. "For two
eight-hour days."

Gran rolled her eyes at Eb. "The human
calculator."

He grinned. "And she doesn't even need batteries."

Gran hugged me then and I could smell the light, sweet scent of her perfume. "Come on. Let's walk around to the other side. I want to see the meadow from over there."

"Reckon I'll water the horses," Eb said to me. He seemed to sense that Gran wanted to be alone with me.

He led the horses away, and Gran and I walked around to the opposite side of the pond and sat down on the edge. The rolling hills, cloaked in dark green, stretched toward the river in the distance. Bees buzzed among the orange and yellow wildflowers still blooming half hidden in the tall grass. Gran took her hat off and fanned her face. "Eb's right. The view from here is wonderful."

"Yes ma'am."

Gran ran her fingers through her short, dark curls. "What do you think, honey? Should we spend the money to bring this old pond back to life, or just let the grasses overtake it?"

I shrugged. "It's your ranch. You should do whatever you want."

"It won't always be mine," she said. "After I'm gone, it'll be yours."

This was a scary piece of news. "Don't talk that way, Gran. You're going to live for a long time."

A playful smile lit her face. "I should hope so. I'd hate to think I sweated through all those aerobics classes for nothing."

I frowned. I couldn't imagine the ranch without her. Most of all, I couldn't imagine myself as an adult and in charge of everything. "What about Mom? And Aunt Gina?"

"Your mother and I have had many conversations about this ranch, my dear. She doesn't want it. And Gina"—Gran clucked her tongue and waved one hand, as if she were swatting an insect—"she's my own flesh and blood, but she doesn't have the sense God gave a goat."

I was still thinking about Mom not wanting the ranch. "How come Mom doesn't want to live here?" I asked. "This is the best place ever."

Gran sighed. "Too many memories, I think. She loved your daddy very much, Jill. Coming back here must be very painful for her. In spite of everything, she still misses him."

Well, I missed him too, and still do, but Mom and I made a pact. We talk about Dad as little as possible. It hurts less that way. Too much talk and we both start remembering the good times and the bad, and then we have to face the fact that he would probably be just as happy never to see either of us again. He sends presents at Christmas and on my birthday, but he hasn't been too eager to have me come visit him. Too busy, he says. I'd just be scared and lonely in a tiny apartment in the middle of Tokyo, waiting for him to come home from work. He's probably right. And I guess I shouldn't complain. As far as I know, he always sends a check when he's supposed to, so at least I don't worry about his picture going up on the walls at the supermarket.

It's funny, but until Gran mentioned it, I'd never really thought about how lonely and sad Mom must feel, even after all this time.

I said to Gran, "Then I guess that's why Mom sends me here by myself."

She nodded. "I expect so. Or at least, that's part of it. I think she's hoping that by traveling alone you'll grow up to be more independent than she was." Gran draped one arm around my shoulders. "Until the day she was married, your mother never set foot outside Travis County."

I pulled a couple of blades of grass and wove them together. "I know that's true," I said. "The part about being independent, I mean. Mom says I shouldn't get married just to have somebody to take care of me."

"She's right about that," Gran said. "Look at me. Widowed before I turned sixty. I've had to learn to manage the ranch, my finances, everything, all by myself."

I stretched out on my back and shaded my eyes with my hat. "Well, you don't have to worry about me. I'm never getting married."

Gran's brows went up. "Is that so? In that case, I guess we'd better put the pond to rights so you'll have some ducks for company when you're old like me and all alone."

"I won't be alone," I said airily. "I'll invite B.J. to live with me."

Her eyes twinkled. "Two old maids living here together, eh? Well, I wouldn't count on that, my dear. Seems to me that Miss B.J. Reynolds has no intention of staying single."

I sat up. "Come on! Don't send out the invitations yet. She's only twelve, Gran."

"Yes, but she's already wearing lipstick and nail polish and curling her hair when it's not even Sunday, as you pointed out. That's not the behavior of a young woman who's planning to live alone."

I sighed. All this talk about the future made me nervous. It seemed too far away to think about, anyway. Anything could happen before I got really old. "Do we have to talk about this now?"

"Yes, we do," she said quietly. "You should know that your mother and I have agreed that the ranch should be left to you. It's already in my will."

"But Gran—"

She held up her hand. "I know. Inheriting the ranch is a huge responsibility. But you're a sensible girl and smart as a whip. I can rest easy knowing that everything your grandfather and I built here will be taken care of after I'm gone."

I stared at her. "Are you sick, Gran?"

"Of course not! I'm healthy as a horse. I just believe in planning ahead, that's all." Her eyes held a faraway look. "Your granddad and I came here right after we were married with twenty-seven dollars and an old Ford. We rented enough land to run some cattle and I worked at the telephone company while he went to law school." She pulled me close to her and ruffled my hair. "Those were the hardest times, and the happiest times, of our lives."

I nodded, my cheek rubbing against the soft fabric of her shirt. "He used to tell me about getting up early to feed the cattle before he went to school."

She laughed softly, remembering. "Oh, how he hated getting up early! Grumbled about it every day of his life, but he always said Texas land is different from land anywhere else. Owning it was worth everything it cost him. I couldn't bear it if it ended up in the hands of strangers."

I smiled up at her, suddenly remembering one of Mrs. Riley's favorite quotes. From Thoreau, I think it is. Something about loving your land more than you love bread and cake. Standing with Gran, knee-deep in the thick summer grass, it wasn't hard to understand how Granddad felt.

We stood quietly for a while, listening to the scolding chatter of the mockingbirds and the hum of insects in the grass. The sun warmed me, and I stretched out again and closed my eyes. After a while, Gran stood up and dusted off the seat of her Levi's. "We'd better find Eb and start back. Those peaches aren't going to jump in the freezer by themselves."

I giggled, imagining the plump fruits jumping in and out of boiling water and into the freezer bags. "I wish they would. It sure would be a lot less trouble."

Gran thought for a moment. "I might let you off the hook today if you'll weed the flower beds tomorrow."

"Deal!" I wanted to ride over to the library and check out some books on astronomy.

"Here comes Eb," Gran said, and we walked around to meet him.

He helped Gran and me mount up, and then he swung into his saddle. From the way he kept glancing at us from beneath his hat brim, I could tell he was dying to know what Gran had decided about the duck pond. But he wasn't about to ask her. We rode for a long time without talking, back along the edge of the meadow, through the stand of trees along the river. When we got back to the barn, we unsaddled the horses and turned them out in the pasture.

"Well," Gran said. "I should get started on those peaches. Thanks for the tour, Eb."

"You're most welcome, Miz Lawrence." Eb leaned against the fence, rubbing Rhett's nose as if he didn't care one way or the other about the duck pond. But the toe of his scuffed boot, jiggling impatiently in the dust, gave him away.

Gran turned around. "By the way, my granddaughter and I have decided to have the pond restored to its former glory. I suggest you get on the phone to that man in Austin and find out when he's coming."

A wide grin split his sun-browned face. "Hot diggity dog!" He jumped in his truck and sped up the road toward his house, leaving Gran and me laughing in the dust.

Chapter Seven

I started on the flower beds early the next morning, while I could still work in the shade. I pulled weeds from under the azalea bushes, listening to the television through the open window. Gran was watching her favorite morning news show while she made another batch of strawberry jam. The smell of warm sugar and strawberries drifted outside, and my mouth watered.

"It'll be seventy-nine and hazy in Los Angeles today," the weatherman predicted.

That reminded me that I hadn't written to Mom in over a week. But if the weatherman hadn't reminded me, Gran would have. She's particular about things like that.

I finished the weeding on one side of the

porch and stood back to admire my work. Freed from the choking weeds, the pink azalea blossoms looked bigger than ever, and the gold and orange marigolds glistened with dew. I moved my tools and the can of liquid fertilizer to the other end of the porch and checked my watch. In another couple of hours, I'd be through with the whole project. Then I could shower and curl up with the books I'd checked out from the library the day before.

I'd found a fantastic book chock-full of star maps and maps of the moon. In the back, all the stars were named in Latin and English. I could hardly wait to read it.

The other book was about Galileo. Mr. Stein had made us do a report on Galileo in science last year, but I wasn't much interested in him then, and I forgot most of what I wrote in my report. What I did remember was that Galileo made his own telescope and discovered mountains on the moon and a bunch of other stuff. Now I wanted to find out more. It's funny how most subjects seem a lot more interesting when nobody is making you learn about them.

Gran came outside dressed in a black linen suit and the pearls Granddad had given her for Christmas one year. She blew me a kiss.

"Where are you going?" I dropped another load of weeds into the wheelbarrow.

"To Austin for a funeral." She fished the keys to the black Lincoln out of her purse. "Mildred Johnson's father passed away Tuesday night."

"Oh." I didn't know what else to say. Death and funerals give me the creeps.

"There's plenty of food in the fridge, and I made a pitcher of lemonade. If you need anything, call B.J.'s mother. They're coming home this morning."

"I'll be okay, Gran. I stay by myself in L.A. all the time."

"Speaking of L.A., don't forget to write to your mother this week."

I grinned. "I won't forget."

She donned her sunglasses. "I probably won't be back till late. I'm giving Helen Mc-Cormick a lift, and she'll be the last one to leave the cemetery." She sighed. "Helen so enjoys a good funeral."

I watched her back the Lincoln out of the garage. She honked the horn and I waved as she started down the road to the highway.

With Gran gone and the television off, it was way too quiet, so I went inside and got my tape player. I popped in a tape and sang along while I pulled weeds and doused the azaleas with fertilizer. That's why I didn't hear B.J. until she tapped me on the shoulder and yelled, "Hey, Jill!"

I jumped, then wheeled around. "Jeez, B.J.! You scared the living daylights out of me!"

"Sorry." She gave me a quick, fierce hug and handed me a package. "I brought you a present."

"A present? How come?"

"No special reason. I just felt like it, that's all."

I dropped my gloves in the dirt and pulled the lid off the little silver box. Inside was a bracelet with a gold charm that said Best Friend.

I lifted it from its cotton nest. "It's beautiful Beej! Thanks!"

B.J. grinned. "You can wear it when you go back to California, to remember me by. Since we can't have matching earrings."

"I really love it," I said, reaching out to hug her again. "I'll wear it every—"

"Hey! Hey, Jill!" Trey came jogging up the road in his cutoffs and sunglasses.

"Trey!" B.J. squealed. In that instant, I vanished from the planet. She took off down the road to meet him, her perfect golden ponytail swinging from side to side as she ran. I raked my hair away from my sweaty forehead and dusted the dirt off my faded shorts.

They came toward the house together, B.J. chattering like a magpie, and Trey hanging on her every word. It was totally disgusting.

Trey pushed his sunglasses to the top of his head. "Whatcha doing?"

"What does it look like?" I snapped. "I'm weeding the flower beds."

"Bummer," Trey said.

"Guess what I did in Dallas?" B.J. said to Trey.

"What?"

"Went to a rock concert."

"You're kidding! Your mom let you go?" I could tell he was impressed. Okay. So was I. But no way was I going to admit it. I knelt in the dirt and dug a few more weeds, just to show her what was really important.

"Mom took me herself." B.J. grinned, crinkling her eyes. "She wore earplugs and read a magazine during the whole thing. Can you imagine?"

"Sounds totally embarrassing to me," Trey said.

B.J. shrugged. "It was either that or miss the concert. I talked some girl into switching seats with me, so I didn't have to sit right next to

Mom. We stood up for the whole thing anyway. It was okay."

"Cool," Trey said.

I couldn't stand it one nanosecond longer. "I saw the Topsies' concert last spring," I said. "They were fantastic."

"The Topsies? Who cares about them? They're for babies," B.J. declared. "Right, Trey?"

"I guess." Trey looked at me. "Dad's helping me set up the telescope on a temporary platform so I won't miss the summer constellations. You can come over some night and look if you want."

I felt as if he had personally handed me the sun, moon and stars. "Great!" I said. "Wait right here."

I flew to my room and grabbed my two library books and took them out to Trey. "Look what I got at the library yesterday."

He flipped through the book of star maps. "I have a copy of this. It's a good book."

I handed him the other one. "Look. Galileo."

B.J. tossed her ponytail. "Oh, Jill, nobody cares about old dead scientists."

She rested one hand on Trey's arm, and I couldn't help noticing her perfect half-moon nails, her perfect pale pink nail polish. I hid my dirty fingernails behind my back.

"I went to a cheerleading clinic last Monday," she said to him. "Watch this."

She lifted both hands high over her head, took a running start and turned a perfect round-off back-handspring, landing in a split. Then she tossed me a long, triumphant look. I held her gaze. Suddenly we seemed caught up in some kind of weird contest. It didn't make sense. Ten minutes ago she'd given me a best-friends bracelet. Now she was trying to make me look like a big fat zero in front of Trey.

"Jill can't do that," she said, getting up off the lawn. "She's not very coordinated."

"Oh, I don't know," I said, supercasual. "Trey taught me to skateboard last week, and I did just fine, huh, Trey."

The look of surprise on her face was definitely worth the skinned knee I'd gotten in the process.

"She did okay," he told B.J.

"Skateboarding's not in anymore, anyway," B.J. said. "Everybody's into in-line skates now. I'm getting some for my birthday next week."

"They're great!" Trey said. "I got a pair last Christmas."

"Cool!" B.J. said. "We can go skating together after Jill goes home. We wouldn't want to run off and leave her behind."

At that moment, I hated B.J. I could feel the blood boiling in my veins. "Don't worry about me," I said evenly. "I can keep up with you. I'll just drive along behind you in Gran's convertible, in case you fall and break your neck or something."

Both of them stared at me.

"You wish!" B.J. said. "You can't drive."

"I can too!"

"Cannot."

"Can too."

"Prove it!" B.J. folded her arms across her chest.

My heart thudded against my ribs. Trey's gaze held mine. I didn't see how I could back down now and ever face him again. I stalled for time.

"I can't right now," I said. "I'm dirty, and I have to finish this flower bed before Gran gets back."

"See?" B.J. said to Trey. "She's just bluffing. I knew she really wouldn't do it because she *can't* do it."

I threw my trowel in the dirt. "All right!" I shouted. "Wait here. I'll show you who's bluffing!"

I tore into the house, stripping off my dirty clothes as I went. A part of me knew I was about to do a stupid and dangerous thing, but it was as if I were standing to one side, watching myself, powerless to stop the chain of events I'd set in motion. I showered and changed in ten minutes flat and came out with my sunglasses and Gran's spare set of keys.

"Want to drive down to the Texas Steakout for a Coke?"

I was scared stiff, but I was not about to let B.J. make a fool of me. Not anymore.

B.J.'s eyes seemed to take up her whole face. "You're not really going to do it."

"Watch me," I said. "You don't have to come if you don't want to. Coming, Trey?"

He dug in the dirt with the toe of his sneaker. "Maybe we'd better not, Jill. I wouldn't want your grandmother to be mad at us."

"She won't be mad. She lets me drive all the time."

"Yeah, right. You don't even have a learner's permit," B.J. pointed out.

"I know, but there's not much traffic out here. When Gran and I go driving, we practically never see a cop. Besides, I'm a very good driver. I don't break the speed limit or anything."

Suddenly I felt cocky. After all, I'd watched Gran drive lots of times, and I'd steered the car down to the highway the day after I got here.

How hard could it be? I walked over to the convertible and slid behind the wheel. "Well, are you coming or not?"

"Come on, Trey," B.J. said. "I bet you ten dollars she chickens out before we get to the highway."

Trey got in beside me and B.J. climbed into the back. I turned the key and the engine purred. I shifted into Drive. "Is everybody ready?"

"Ready!" Trey said.

"Let's go," B.J. said. "If we're going."

I let out on the brake and the car rolled down the gravel drive. Once we actually started moving, I lost my nerve. I waited till the car slowed nearly to a stop, then barely tapped the accelerator. We bounced along the road. I gripped the steering wheel, hoping I looked more confident than I felt.

"There's a big pothole right down here," I said. My voice sounded high and strange in my ears. "I almost hit it back when I was just learning to drive."

We got to the highway. I coasted to a stop at the intersection and looked up and down the road. My mouth felt dry as cotton. I could hear the blood pulsing in my ears. Sweat trickled down my back.

"Well?" B.J. leaned forward and I could feel her warm breath on the back of my neck. "Are we going to the Steakout or are we just going to sit here in the sun all day, broiling like chickens?"

"We're going," I said, and I stepped on the gas. The car shot across the highway and into the far lane. I jerked the wheel back to the left.

"Hey, careful Jill!" Trey braced his hands against the dashboard.

"Sorry." I pressed the accelerator. It seemed as if we were going at least a hundred miles an hour.

B.J. leaned forward again. "Twenty-five miles an hour? I can *run* faster than that!"

"Then why don't you?" I shouted at her, without taking my eyes off the highway. "I'll just pull over right here and you can jog the rest of the way."

Trey turned around in his seat. "Just shut up, Belinda! You're making her nervous."

That was the understatement of the century. I was so scared now that I didn't see how I'd be able to swallow a single sip of Coke, even if we made it to the Steakout alive.

Trey settled back in his seat. "This is neat, Jill," he said. "And what a great day for a drive in the country!"

I could tell he was trying to look relaxed so I wouldn't get more nervous. I could have hugged him, except I didn't dare take my hands off the wheel. After what seemed like a hundred years, we came to the Texas Steakout. I slowed to a crawl and started to turn in to the parking lot.

"Wait!" Trey yelled.

I stomped on the brake just as a cement truck roared past. I sat there in the middle of the highway, too terrified to move. The turn signal made a little clicking sound, blinking on and off. An empty cattle truck rattled past us without even slowing down.

"You can turn now," Trey said. "The coast is clear."

I pulled into the parking lot and took up two spaces right by the door. I shut the engine off and took the keys out of the ignition. My legs had turned to rubber. I turned around in my seat, pushed my sunglasses to the top of my head and smiled brightly at B.J. "See? Nothing to it. Don't forget, you owe Trey ten dollars."

We went inside and took a booth at the back. We ordered Cokes and listened to the music blaring from the jukebox. Trey took some quarters from his pocket.

"Want to pick out some songs, Belinda?"

She tossed her head and wrinkled her nose. "All they have here is goat-roper music."

He went over to the jukebox and picked out some songs. We were safe for now, but I still faced that long drive back to the ranch. Just thinking about it made my stomach hurt.

I took tiny sips of my Coke so it would last

a long time. B.J. and Trey didn't talk much. We listened to the music and watched the other people in the restaurant. After a while, the waitress came by and put our check on the table. Another half hour passed. We had finished our Cokes and eaten all the crushed ice out of the bottoms of the glasses. Trey had fed his last quarter to the jukebox. The waitress kept giving us the kind of look Mr. Stein used in science class when he knew we weren't working on our lab experiments.

"Let's go," B.J. said. "This is boring."

Trey nodded. "I gotta go, Jill. Dad will be looking for me."

"Okay," I said, being supercasual again. I paid for the Cokes and stood up. "Ready when you are."

We started for the door. When I pushed against it, the man on the other side jerked it open so fast that I nearly lost my balance. I looked up. It was Eb.

Chapter Eight

Eb smiled at me and tipped his brown Stetson as if it were the most natural thing in the world for him to run into me at the Steakout. His eyes flickered to the car keys in my hand. "Hey there, kiddo."

"Hey, Eb." I stepped outside to let some people in, and B.J. and Trey came out. I swallowed. Any minute now, Eb was bound to ask where Gran was, and my goose would be cooked when he found out I'd driven the Mustang by myself.

Eb squinted at Trey. "You must be Professor Wilborn's boy."

"Yes sir." Trey was scared, too. Whether for me or for himself, though, I couldn't tell.

"You 'bout finished building that house?"

"Yes sir," Trey said again. "Dad wants to move in before school starts."

Eb nodded and said to B.J. "How are *you*, Miss Belinda? Your folks doing all right?"

"Yes sir," B.J. said.

I bet Eb had never been called "sir" so many times in one day in his whole life.

Eb's dark gaze rested on mine. "I'm glad I happened by here," he said. "I thought that was your car in the parking lot, and I says to myself, I'll bet a hundred dollars that girl went off without her glasses again."

He turned to Trey and B.J. "She's not s'posed to drive without her glasses, but nine times outta ten, she forgets them."

My mouth fell open and I stared into Eb's face. My eyesight has always been just perfect, but I nodded, too confused to speak.

"So," Eb went on, "I says to myself, I'd best stop in and see if I can drive that convertible back to the ranch for Miss Jill, before she gets into all kinds of trouble by not having her glasses on."

He pushed his hat to the back of his head, winked at Trey and spoke to him as if I were on another planet. "You have no idea how much store Miz Lawrence puts in that little car. Wouldn't do for Miss Jill to put a scratch on it 'cause she couldn't see where she's a-going."

"No sir," Trey said.

B.J. stared at me. "I never knew you wore glasses, Jill!"

I shrugged. I didn't want to lie to B.J., but I couldn't let Eb down, either. Not after he'd gone to so much trouble to save my pride. Not to mention my life.

Weak with relief, I handed him the keys. "Thanks Eb," I said, smooth as churned butter. "I'm really glad you came along. Gran would have never forgiven me if I'd dented up her car."

"That's a fact." He opened the car door and we piled in. I sat in front beside Eb, and B.J. and Trey got in the back. Eb backed the Mustang out of the parking lot and we headed up the highway. I scrunched down in the seat, watching the traffic and the scenery flash by. Normally, I try not to attract God's attention, but that day I prayed that Eb and I would beat Gran home from Austin and that I could finish weeding the flower beds before she got back from the funeral. I promised God that if He'd just let me out of this horrible mess I'd gotten myself into, I'd never even sit behind the wheel of a car till I was thirty. Maybe thirty-five.

We dropped B.J. and Trey off at the Hallaby place and took the shortcut across the north edge of the pasture, headed for home. The Mustang jounced along the rutted dirt road, past the peach orchard still heavy with fruit, and up the grassy rise to the house.

God must have been busy elsewhere while I was praying, because as soon as we rounded the bend in the road, I saw Gran standing on the porch, still wearing her black suit. Granddad's Lincoln stood in the drive.

"Uh-oh," Eb said. "Looks like we're in a whole lot of trouble."

I nodded, feeling miserable. "I'm sorry, Eb."

He shook his head. "I'm not the one you've got to apologize to. I know your granny. She's bound to pitch a major fit."

"I know."

We continued up the road. "Thanks for making up that story about my glasses," I said. "And for bringing us back home."

He raked his hand through his hair. "Generally speaking, I don't believe in lying. But I could see you'd got yourself into a bad fix. No sense making it worse in front of your friends. I expect you learned your lesson."

Eb pulled into the driveway and shut off the engine. We got out. He jammed his Stetson onto his head and dropped the car keys into Gran's outstretched hand. "Miz Lawrence."

"Thank you, Eb." Her voice was as hard as granite, her expression as dark as a Texas thundercloud.

Eb shot me a sympathetic look and said to Gran, "I'd better check on Rhett. He threw a shoe yesterday and his foot's kinda sore."

"Yes," said Gran. "You do that."

Eb headed for the pasture, his boots crunching on the gravel driveway. Gran took me by the hand and propelled me into the house. We faced each other on the sofa in the living room.

"Now then, young lady. Suppose you explain yourself. Trey Wilborn's mother called here nearly hysterical when he told her what the three of you have been up to today."

"I'm sorry, Gran," I began.

I explained about B.J. and the rock concert and her stupid cheerleading stunts and her new skates. I told her about Trey's inviting me to look through the telescope and how B.J. made fun of my astronomy books and how she'd said the Topsies were for babies and how I'd almost *had* to drive the Mustang to prove I wasn't a total idiot.

When I finished, it was so quiet in the room I could hear Gran's breathing. It was quick and deep, as if she'd just finished doing her aerobics and hadn't cooled down yet. Finally she said, "Do you realize what a foolish thing you've done? You might have been killed! All of you!"

"I know, Gran." I shuddered at the memory of the speeding cement truck. "I'm really sorry."

"You *should* be. I'm disappointed in you, Jill. I'd never have believed you'd do something so utterly irresponsible."

I waited. I knew more was coming. Finally Gran said, her voice very low and precise, "For the next seven days you will not leave this house. You will do your chores and write to your mother and help me in the orchard. You may not watch television and you may not listen to your tapes. . . ."

There were more "you-may-nots" but my mind shut down shortly after she said "seven days," because B.J.'s thirteenth birthday party was six days away. I hadn't missed one of her parties since we were in kindergarten.

"What about B.J.'s party?" I said.

"What about it?"

"It's next Tuesday, Gran. That's in six days."

"So it is," she said. "It's a shame you'll have to miss it."

My throat swelled and ached, and tears started behind my eyes. "Please, Gran," I begged. "Let me go to the party, and I'll serve extra days to make up for it."

She shook her head. "I'm sorry, my dear. This is one party you're going to miss."

"But why?"

"To remind you of the seriousness of what you did today! You took three precious lives in your hands. You could have caused three families untold grief."

"But nothing happened! Eb took care of us."

"Next time you might not be so lucky." She stood up. "Go to your room and stay there until suppertime. I'll tell you when you may come out."

"But—"

"Now, Jill." Her eyes glittered like two black diamonds.

I stomped down the hall and slammed the door so hard the whole house rattled. Sure, I deserved to be punished, but I didn't deserve to miss my best friend's birthday party. Even if it *was* her fault that I was in this trouble in the first place. If she hadn't acted so superior about her stupid concerts and her stupid cheerleading, I wouldn't have felt like I had to do something as spectacular as driving the car to keep up with her.

Suddenly I missed Mom and L.A. and Aunt Gina. I even missed my wet, squalling cousin. I didn't care if I ever saw Texas or Gran or the ranch or B.J. ever again. I pulled my suitcases from under the bed and opened all the drawers and closets. I ripped my clothes off their hangers and stuffed them into the suitcases. I figured I had enough cash to take a taxi into Austin and from there I would call Mom and have her charge an airline ticket for me. I had almost finished with the second suitcase when Gran opened the door.

She took one look at my luggage and said, "And where do you think you're going?"

"Home." I made my voice as hard and cold as ice. "And don't try to stop me."

"Oh, I'm not going to stop you," Gran said. "I'll be perfectly happy for you to go. But not for seven days."

I stared at her through a red haze. "I hate you!" I shouted. "And I hate this stupid ranch. When you die it can go to the rats for all I care!"

She winced, but she said quietly, "I'm sorry you feel that way. But I'd rather you hate me and the ranch than to think you can run away from the consequences of your behavior."

She sounded just like the guidance counselor at my school. Mr. Richards was always talking about rules and consequences.

Gran folded her arms across her chest. "It seems to me that you and B.J. haven't been getting along all that well this summer anyway. Perhaps a week apart will be good for both of you."

She pulled something from her pocket and I saw that it was the silver bracelet box. "I found this on the porch. I believe it's yours."

She dropped it onto my bed and turned to go. "As soon as you've put your things away, you may come to supper. We're having roast beef and corn on the cob."

"I'm not hungry."

"Suit yourself." She closed the door.

I dumped my suitcases on the floor and stretched out on the bed, staring at the patch of blue sky beyond my window. The late afternoon sun slanted through the trees, casting shifting patterns of light onto the pink patchwork quilt. I felt too defeated and too lonely to cry. Deep down I knew that Gran was right to punish me, but I still didn't see why I had to miss B.J.'s party. The thought of her laughing and opening her presents and, worst of all, flirting with Trey while I was imprisoned at the ranch made me furious. The way Gran was treating me was mean. Cruel. Probably even illegal.

Seven days without TV or tapes or the telephone! She might as well have said seven years. Seven *hundred* years. Already I felt restless. I got up and paced the room, picking up books and pictures and putting them down again. Then I caught sight of my reflection in the mirror.

For some reason, my hair looked better than it had all year, full and shiny and shot with streaks of gold from the sun. My skin had tanned enough that my freckles had almost disappeared. I turned sideways and stood up straight. Was it my imagination, or did my chest look fuller than it had at the start of the summer? I picked up Gran's silver-handled brush and swept my hair into a smooth ponytail and held it in place with my hands. Suddenly my face had angles and curves I'd never noticed before. My eyes seemed darker and larger, too. For the first time in my life, I felt pretty. It was weird, looking at my reflection and liking what I saw. I wet my lips and smiled into the mirror and it came to me then what to do with myself during my exile.

I would embark on a crash program of self-improvement. I would brush my hair a hundred strokes every day. I would polish my nails, wash my face twice a day, and think of witty things to say to Trey. I might have to miss B.J.'s party, but the Fourth of July was only ten days away, and when I showed up for the parade and the band concert down on the river, C.J. Mussleman and Sons wouldn't be the only ones setting off fireworks.

Chapter Nine

The days crawled by. Every morning I got up early and did fifty sit-ups and brushed my hair before having breakfast in the kitchen with Gran. Every morning she smiled pleasantly and made conversation while we ate, but she never once went back on her word. The television stayed silent, and my tape player stayed locked in her closet. I guess B.J. and Trey had been told not to call me, because the phone rang only once and it was a salesman from Austin wanting Gran to buy aluminum siding for the house. Even Eb stayed away. Once I saw him riding Scarlett, and several times I heard his pickup rattling down the road, rock music blaring through the open windows. I wondered whether Gran was mad at him for his part in my escapade, but I never brought it up.

On Tuesday, the day of B.J.'s party, Gran handed me a plate of scrambled eggs and ham and poured some orange juice. "I'm going to Austin this afternoon," she said. "If you like, I'll drop off your present for B.J. on the way."

"That's okay," I said. "I'd rather wait till I can give it to her myself." I sipped my orange juice and picked up my fork.

She studied me over the rim of her coffee cup. For a split second I thought she might change her mind and let me go to the party after all, but then she said, "Sweetie, I am truly sorry about today, but I hope you understand my reasons."

I shrugged. While I was grounded I'd gotten so used to the idea of missing the party that it no longer bothered me that much. Gran was right about one thing. B.J. and I weren't getting along all that well. Everything about this summer was different. More complicated. We no longer seemed like two peas in a pod.

Gran took her plate to the sink and turned on the faucet. With her back to me, she said, "The excavators are coming today to dig out the duck pond. You may go watch if you like, but I expect you back here by four o'clock."

Not much of a reprieve, but it was better than nothing. The pond was, after all, still on our ranch, and so well hidden that I wasn't likely to see another living soul while I was out there. I guess Gran knew if I had to read one more mystery I might lose my mind.

As soon as Gran left for Austin, I went out to the barn and gave Scarlett a lump of sugar. She stamped and tossed her head and flicked her tail while I saddled her.

We took the same path Gran and Eb and I had taken before. The sun was out, but I could see clouds building to the north and west and I made a mental note to keep an eye on them. Summer storms in Texas can turn violent in the twinkling of an eye.

Scarlett picked her way along the riverbank

and I just sat back in the saddle and breathed the summer air. On the opposite side of the river, the honeysuckle still blossomed, making the air smell as sweet as Gran's Sunday-morning perfume.

"Whoa, Scarlett." I slid from the saddle, kicked off my shoes and waded across the river to the other side. Sand squished up between my toes and the water ran clear and cold over my feet. I pulled off a bunch of the honey-suckle vines, stuck one behind my ear, and draped the rest around Scarlett's neck. She tossed her head and nickered and I laughed out loud, appreciating my freedom.

I heard the roar of heavy machinery even before we got to the pond. We came up over the last rise and saw an orange backhoe lum-bering back and forth along the edge of the pond. Leaving Scarlett to graze in the shade, I slid into my sneakers and jogged across the meadow.

The man on the backhoe waved to me, and his helper jumped out of his pickup and came over to where I stood. "You can't stand here, hon. Too dangerous."

"This is my gran's ranch," I said. "This was my duck pond when I was little."

"That's real nice, but I have to ask you to move. Go back over there with your horse."

"I can't see from there," I said. I don't know why I suddenly felt so stubborn.

He sighed and turned back to the pickup. He pulled out a hard hat and thrust it into my hands. "Here, then. Put this on. But for the love of Pete, stay out of Ben's way."

"Thanks." I grinned at him and he touched the brim of his own hard hat in a little salute and went back to studying his charts. I wandered around to the far end of the meadow and watched the backhoe dump the dirt into a waiting truck. Watching the duck pond take shape again gave me the funniest feeling. It was as if I could actually see me and Mom and Dad and Gran and Granddad and Aunt Gina the way we were when I was little and we were all safe and happy. I could almost hear Dad's quiet laughter floating out of the velvet darkness and Granddad's songs riding the night wind up to the stars. I scooped up a dirt clod and let the warm earth sift through my fingers.

I remembered what Gran had said about Granddad, how hard he'd worked to buy the ranch and how important it was to hold on to it, no matter what. And how, someday, it would be mine to cherish and protect. Suddenly the wide, grassy meadows, the dark shapes of the cattle against the bright blue Texas sky, the very earth itself, seemed different. More alive. I was ashamed of the remark I'd made to Gran about not wanting the ranch. Granddad was right. It was worth whatever it cost to keep it.

I stood as close as I dared to the edge of the pond, the smell of damp earth and summer hay mingling in my nostrils. By next year the pond would be full of life again, teeming with ducks and wild lilies and a dozen kinds of insects. Maybe even a few fish.

The backhoe shuddered to a stop. Ben, the driver, jumped from the cab and jogged over to the pickup. Then the other man, the one who'd given me the hard hat, waved to me and motioned me toward the truck. At that same moment, thunder rumbled in the distance and I glanced up.

The sky had turned the color of an old bruise. Heavy, greenish-black clouds boiled up directly overhead. The wind blew suddenly cold, stirring the leaves of the trees. The air around me filled with the musty smell of coming rain. I took off at a dead run back across the meadow to where Scarlett stood pawing at the ground. I leaped into the saddle and turned the horse for home, racing across the north end of the pasture along the old dirt trail, one eye on the low-hanging branches that whipped in the wind, the other on the darkening sky.

We were in sight of the house when the first torrent of cold rain swept over the meadow. Thunder rolled, shaking the ground beneath us. Lightning danced across the horizon, and

Scarlett shied and nickered. I dug my heels into her sides, urging her on. The rain beat down, soaking my shirt and filling my shoes. Scarlett's wet hair prickled my bare legs as we sprinted along the muddied trail.

When we reached the barn, I unsaddled the horse and rubbed her down till she was dry. I gave her a bucket of oats and filled her water trough and led her into the stall. Spooked by the storm, Rhett tossed his head and danced sideways in his stall. I rubbed his face, crooning softly to calm him.

Outside, a car horn sounded. I picked up my wet knapsack and dashed from the barn to the shelter of the front porch.

Gran pulled the car into the garage and opened the door.

"Hi, honey!" she called. "Mercy me! You look like a drowned rat. Come give me a hand."

I helped her into the house with her shopping bags and two boxes from Tenniger's department store. We dropped everything on the living room sofa. Gran's face glowed with that special light she gets after an especially fruitful day of shopping.

"Jeez, Gran, looks like you cleaned out every store in Austin."

"I tried," she said, mock-serious. "But there was one chartreuse pantsuit that just didn't do a thing for me."

She studied me for a minute and then burst out laughing. "What is that thing on your head?"

The hard hat! I'd completely forgotten it. I explained to Gran.

"Well," she said, "I guess you can take it back to them tomorrow." She tossed her purse and keys on the coffee table. "I don't know about you, but I could do with a cup of tea."

She started for the kitchen. "Get out of those wet clothes before you catch your death of cold."

I went to my room and changed into dry clothes and set the hard hat on the windowsill so I wouldn't forget to return it. When I got back to the kitchen, Gran had set the table for two, with a lace tablecloth and her best gold-and-white china. A plate of tea cakes and a bowl of fresh strawberries and cream waited on the counter.

"I loved taking tea when I was a girl," Gran said. "My aunt Libby used to take me to tea at the Driscoll Hotel. All the ladies wore their nicest dresses and little hats and white gloves." She smiled at the memory. "It was quite elegant."

She poured the tea and the rich, spicy smell drifted across the kitchen. I sipped my tea and munched on a lemon-flavored cake. The rain fell harder. Thunder rolled and crashed, rattling the windows in their frames. The lights flickered and went out.

Gran found the emergency candles and lit them, filling the room with dancing light and dim shadows. In the kitchen we felt cozy and safe, sitting shoulder to shoulder at the table, our voices sounding small in the cavernous room.

I told her about the pond and the honey-suckle I'd seen along the river, and how beautiful the ranch seemed to me now. "I love it here, Gran," I said. "And I'm sorry about what I said the other day. About not wanting the ranch."

She patted my hand. "I knew you didn't mean it. And I can't think of anything that would make me happier than to know you're living here on Lawrence land with your children and grandchildren."

"That's a long way off," I said.

"I hope so, but knowing that everything is in order is still a comfort to me."

She finished her tea and we turned on the portable radio and listened to the weather report.

When it was over, Gran said, "Well, it doesn't sound too bad. The river may rise farther downstream, but I don't think we're in any danger."

We sat for another half hour, listening to the steady beat of rain on the roof and the rush of wind through the trees. At last the lights flickered and came back on, and Gran stood up and led me to the pile of packages in the living room.

"Wait till you see what I bought," she said, smiling down at me.

She took the lid off the first box and held up a soft pink linen dress with a scalloped hem and scooped neck. "Well?"

My heart sank. "It's . . . pretty, Gran," I said, "but don't you think it looks too old for me?"

She hooted. "Of course it's too old for you, silly. It's mine! For my birthday next month." She held it up in front of her and twirled around like a ballerina. "I might be old, but I'm not stupid. I know better than to buy something like this for a teenager!"

She draped the dress over the back of the sofa and handed me the other box. "This one's yours."

I took the top off the box and lifted the dress from its tissue-paper nest. "Oh, Gran!"

Usually I'd rather get a root canal than

wear a dress, but this was the prettiest one I'd ever seen. It was pale blue with a straight skirt and bell sleeves. It didn't have a sash or acres of lace like the dresses Mom usually buys for me. It was perfect. I couldn't wait for B.J. to see it.

Gran's eyes shone. "That color is just right for you." She picked up a shoe box. "I got you these to go with it."

I took out a pair of white slippers with tiny heels.

Then she cleared her throat and handed me a small white bag with fancy gold letters on it. "Here's one more thing."

I opened it up and almost died of embarrassment.

"It's a bra," Gran said, when I took it out of the sack.

"I can see that. But Gran, I don't—"

"It's time. I realized it the other day when you wore that blue T-shirt I gave you last summer."

I felt my face redden. I dropped my shoulders and hunched forward. "I'm flat as a board," I said, even though I'd seen for myself that I wasn't quite that flat. Still, the idea that anybody else had noticed was mortifying.

A smile played on her lips. "Stand up straight. And then go look in the mirror. You're not flat as a board anymore."

Right then, I started crying. I got started and couldn't stop. I shoved the empty boxes, the mounds of tissue paper off the couch and threw myself against the pillows. I beat my fists and wailed as if Gran were beating the very stuffing out of me.

Maybe it was nerves. Maybe I felt worse about missing B.J.'s party than I wanted to admit. Mostly I felt like my whole life was hurtling along like a runaway train, and I was powerless to stop it.

Gran perched on the edge of the sofa and wrapped her arms around me. She didn't lecture me or tell me to stop. She just rocked me back and forth, the way she did when I was little and got a scraped knee or a bee sting.

After a while I calmed down and the tears finally stopped.

Gran kissed the top of my head. "Well," she murmured against my hair. "It seems we've weathered two storms tonight."

She got up and said something about washing the dishes. I scooped up my new dress, the shoes and the gold-and-white bag from the lingerie store. I put everything away in my closet—except the bra. I folded it, white bag and all, into a tiny square and stuffed it in the back of my sock drawer, underneath a stack of magazines and my bag of lucky marbles. As far as I was concerned, it could stay there the rest of the summer. The rest of my life, even.

Chapter Ten

Around here, the Fourth of July is a big deal. For weeks before the day actually arrives, the newspaper runs stories about the barbecue down at Travis Park, the bands, the watermelon-eating contest, the ice-cream social, the parade, and the big fireworks display on the river.

The store owners in town put up red, white and blue streamers over their doorways, and the chamber of commerce supplies flags for every street corner. The grocery store advertises specials on hot dogs, buns and soft drinks and gives away red, white and blue balloons to every kid under age ten.

I'm too old for the balloons now, but I still look forward to celebrating with Gran every year.

We got up early on the fourth and had breakfast in the kitchen. I had just poured my second glass of milk when Eb ambled in. It was the first time I'd seen him up close since he drove the convertible back from the Texas Steakout for me.

If Gran was mad at him for it, she didn't show it. She said, "Good morning, Eb! Isn't it a beautiful day for a parade?" Her smile was as bright as the heavy silver earrings dangling from her ear lobes.

"Yes ma'am, it surely is." He tossed his hat on a chair and pulled out the one next to mine, rattling the empty coffee cup at his place. He winked at me. "Hey there, kiddo."

"Hi." It had been ten whole days since my mortifying episode with the car, but looking him in the eye made me feel ashamed all over again. I concentrated on what was left of my French toast and strawberries.

Gran poured herself a fresh cup of coffee and one for Eb.

"Thank you, Miz Lawrence." He stirred in

the sugar and cream. "Y'all going down to the parade this morning?"

"Wouldn't miss it for all the tea in China," Gran said. "You coming, Eb?"

He shook his head. "No ma'am. I'm headed to San Antone."

I looked up, stunned at the sudden disappointment welling up inside me. Before, Eb had seemed like a big brother, but the flutterings going on inside me now didn't feel at all sisterly. I watched his smile travel from his eyes to his lips and back again and I realized for the first time how beautiful he was.

Gran made a little sound in her throat, and I jumped, feeling the color rise in my cheeks.

"Try to make it back for the fireworks, Eb," Gran said. "It won't seem like the Fourth without you."

"Thank you, ma'am. I'll do my best." He finished his coffee and stood up. "I should get going."

"Don't forget your hat!" I blurted—then I felt like a total fool.

"Why thank you, Miss Jill." He smiled at me, and I couldn't help noticing that his teeth were so white and even that he could have sold toothpaste in a magazine ad. I got that funny feeling again, deep in the pit of my stomach, as if a Ping-Pong game were going on down there. What was the matter with me?

He picked up his hat and started for the door.

Gran said, "If you get back in time, meet us at the park by the baseball diamond. That's the best place to watch the fireworks."

"Will do. Bye."

"Bye, Eb!" I sang. I felt as light as air.

"Hmm," said Gran.

"What?" I picked up my empty plate and took it to the sink.

She looked thoughtful for a moment, then said, "Nothing. Go get changed while I load the dishwasher. We want to get downtown in time to get a good seat for the parade."

I went to my room and took out the navy-and-white shorts set Mom had sent from California. I started to slip the top over my head, then stopped. I turned sideways and checked the mirror, and in that moment I thought of Eb and how great he looked in his pressed Levi's and red cotton shirt. A weird warmth flowed through me like . . . I don't know what it was like. It was totally different from anything I'd ever felt before. All I know is that the next minute, I was fishing my new bra out of the bottom of my sock drawer.

I put it on, got dressed and brushed my hair a hundred extra strokes, hoping Eb would show up in time to see the fireworks.

Gran knocked on the door and stuck her head in. "Ready, hon?"

"Just a minute." I twisted my hair into a ponytail and fastened it with a red, white and blue ribbon.

"Hubba hubba," Gran said. "Hold everything while I call Hollywood. I think I'm living with a genuine movie star."

I grinned and twirled around for her inspection.

Her dark eyes twinkled. "Couldn't be you're trying to impress Trey Wilborn, could it?"

I felt the color steal across my face again. "Not really," I said. "You said yourself it never hurts to look your best."

"So I did." She dug through her purse for her keys and we went out to the garage. She grinned down at me. "I'll bet Trey won't believe it's really you."

"It's only been a little over a week, Gran. I haven't changed *that* much."

"If you say so." She unlocked the car doors. "Hop in. Let's make tracks."

We drove to town, parked in the gravel lot behind the drug store and cut through the alley to Main Street. A crowd had gathered, awaiting the start of the parade. Mr. Davis, the principal at my old school, waved at me, and I waved back. The couple who ran the bakery on Elm had staked out a choice spot beneath a tree, complete with lawn chairs and a cooler.

"Looks as if Mr. and Mrs. Salzman are here to stay," Gran remarked. She nudged me with her elbow. "Look, there's the new minister, Reverend Carson, and his wife. Have you met them yet, Jill?"

"No ma'am."

Gran started to cross the street but changed her mind. "Oh well, I guess it can wait. He's very nice and his wife is quite charming; she teaches piano three days a week and volunteers at the hospital in Austin on Tuesdays and Thursdays. I'm sure I couldn't manage a schedule like that."

I was about to say that ranching was ten times harder than giving piano lessons, but just then two boys from my old school, Bruce Swearingen and Stanley Voss, pushed through the crowd, shooting at each other with giant water pistols.

Bruce had grown taller, but he still wore his same brushy crew cut and baggy shorts. Stanley was the same old skinny, cow-eyed Stanley, following Bruce around like a lost puppy.

"Gotcha!" Bruce yelled.

"Did not!" Stanley skirted the Salzmans'

lawn chairs and dashed along the sidewalk to-ward Gran and me, brandishing his neon-orange water pistol.

"Did so. Take that! And that!"

A stream of cold water hit me squarely in the face and dribbled down the front of my new blouse. "Bruce Swearingen, you lame-brained idiot!" I screamed.

"Oh, for heaven's sake!" Gran opened her purse and handed me a tissue. I wiped my face and blotted the spot on my blouse. The fabric was so wet that the lace on my bra showed through. I could feel my face turning red. I wished for the ground to open up and swallow me.

"Bruce Swearingen, freeze!" A woman's voice rose above the crowd noise, and heads turned. Bruce's mother pushed through the knot of people gathered on the corner and came over to where he stood, not ten feet from me. Grabbing the water pistol in one hand and the back of Bruce's neck in the other, she marched him over to us.

"Apologize to these ladies!"

"Sorry," Bruce mumbled.

"Well, I should think you would be!" Gran sounded exactly like Mrs. Riley. "Those things are dangerous, Bruce. Especially in a crowd like this."

"I told him to leave it at home, but you know kids," Mrs. Swearingen said. "The minute your back is turned . . ." Her voice trailed off and then she looked at me. "Are you okay, hon?"

"I guess so," I said to the ground.

Gran put her arm around me. "In this heat, I'm sure she'll dry out in no time."

"Well, I'm really sorry," Mrs. Swearingen said. "I guess I'm going to have to put this one in a cage until I can civilize him. Come on, Bruce."

I felt Bruce's eyes on me and looked up. He was staring right at my chest. He waited till his mother moved off, then he turned back to me. "Nice boobs, Jill," he drawled under his breath.

"Curl up and die," I muttered.

"Pardon?" said a voice at my elbow.

I looked up into the puzzled face of Reverend Carson. "Excuse me," I said, and bolted to the other side of the street.

I stood behind a lamppost and waited for the parade to begin. Across the street, Gran was deep in conversation with the minister. Stanley Voss had climbed onto the second floor of the Kut 'N' Kurl beauty shop, where he had a clear shot at anybody passing below. He wore a red-and-blue Texas Rangers baseball cap turned backwards on his head and a pair of cutoff jeans so baggy he had to hitch them up every time he moved. Poor Stanley. Dumb as a box of rocks. But at least he wasn't mean and rude like Bruce.

Music sounded and the crowd quieted. Heads turned toward the far end of Main Street. The parade came into view, led by the high school band, their bright brass instruments flashing in the sunlight. Two majorettes carried a banner that said "Pride of the Lone

Star State." Next came the Texas flag, its one white star gleaming bright against red and blue. Behind the band came the mayor in a red convertible. His bald head had turned pink in the hot sun, and he had rolled up the sleeves of his white shirt and loosened his tie. His wife, in a pink-and-white dress, held a white parasol over her head and turned from side to side, waving to the crowd.

Next came a Volkswagen full of clowns, and then the sheriff's posse on horseback. The horses' hooves made hollow sounds on the pavement. Their silver trappings jingled with every step.

The crowd whistled and clapped when the posse rode by.

"There you are," said a voice, and I turned around to find Trey grinning down at me.

"Hi," I said, stealing a glance at the damp spot on my blouse.

"Hi."

Then we ran out of things to say. A group of gymnastics students wearing black tights and leotards cartwheeled down the street. Men in military uniforms marched by. Applause rippled up and down the street.

"Nice parade," Trey finally said.

"Yeah, but the fireworks show is the best part," I said. "C.J. Mussleman and Sons puts on the biggest show in Texas. You coming?"

He nodded. "After the buildup Belinda gave it, I wouldn't dare miss it."

"Where is she, anyway?" I craned my neck, searching the crowd for her familiar blond ponytail. "I thought for sure she'd come by my house this morning."

Trey squinted at me. "She went to Austin with her folks. Said she'd be back for the fireworks, though."

Jealousy stabbed at my insides. B.J. was *my* best friend. How come Trey was the one who always knew where she was and what she was doing?

"At least she could've called me," I said. "I haven't seen her in over a week."

He shrugged. "You'll see her tonight."

I kicked at a loose stone on the sidewalk. "How was the birthday party?"

"Okay, I guess. Nothing special." He grinned. "Bruce gave her a roll of toilet paper with little red hearts all over it. She threw it at him, and it almost landed in the punch bowl and her mother made her apologize in front of everybody."

We turned back to the parade. Down the street came the high school cheerleaders in their royal blue-and-gold uniforms. Sue Ellen Coates, my former babysitter, turned a perfect cartwheel right in the middle of the street and waved to the crowd. They cheered and whistled and stomped their feet on the pavement. Sue Ellen caught my eye and winked as she went by.

"Wow, she's really something," Trey said. "Do you know her?"

I didn't know whether to be pleased that I knew Sue Ellen or mad at Trey for pointing out how gorgeous she was.

"She was my babysitter back in third grade,"

I said. "She's practically eighteen now. Much too old for you."

Trey laughed out loud. "Are you always so blunt?"

"It's the truth," I said.

"Jill, chill out. I know she's not interested in me. I just think she's pretty, that's all."

He stared at me until I felt my face redden. "Come to think of it, you're not bad either. What have you done to yourself? You look different."

My heart nearly jumped out of my chest, but I tried to stay cool. I tossed my ponytail the way I'd seen B.J. do it. "I just put my hair up is all."

"Oh." He jammed his hands into his pockets. "Want to hang out together? We could go over to the picnic grounds and watch the watermelon-eating contest."

"Sure!" I thought I might burst from sheer, unexpected happiness. "Wait here. I'll go ask Gran."

I jogged across the street just in front of

another group of clowns and found Gran and the minister's wife standing in the shade of the hardware store, fanning themselves with pieces of cardboard from an empty popcorn box.

"There are you, dear," Gran said. "Come and meet Mrs. Carson." Gran drew me forward. "This is my granddaughter, Jill."

"Hi, sweet thing," drawled Mrs. Carson. "Enjoying the parade?"

"Yes ma'am," I said. "Gran, may Trey and I go watch the watermelon-eating contest?"

She glanced across the street and back to me. "I suppose so, but don't leave the park without telling me."

"I won't!"

Just as I started to cross Main Street, I heard a loud grinding noise. Somebody yelled, "Oh no!" and then everything went black.

Chapter Eleven

When I woke up it was dark outside, but the strange room seemed way too bright. I blinked. My left arm felt heavy, my feet icy. Gran hovered above me, her expression anxious.

"Jill? Sweetie? Can you hear me?"

My mouth felt dry but I managed to say, "Hi, Gran."

A woman in white came over, and then I realized where I was. The hospital.

"What happened?" I tried to sit up.

With strong hands, the nurse held me to the bed. "Lie still, sugar."

The door opened and a doctor in a blue scrub suit came in and shined a tiny flashlight into my eyes. He switched it off and smiled at Gran. "Her pupils are dilating normally. That's a good sign."

Gran breathed a sigh of relief. "Thank God."

"What happened?" I asked again.

"Seems you tangled with the fire department's new engine," the doctor explained.

"It wasn't the driver's fault," Gran said. "There was no way he could have stopped in time. Luckily, he was barely moving."

"I didn't even see him coming," I said. "Can I have some water?"

The nurse handed me a glass of ice cubes. "This will have to do for now." She shook her head and the little gold pin on her cap glittered in the light. "How could you not see a fire truck?"

I crunched on the ice cubes and lay back against the pillows. "I was thinking about something else, I guess."

The adults laughed, but it was a laugh of relief.

Gran took my hand and said to the doctor. "When may I take her home?"

"Let's keep her here overnight. If there are no complications, I'll dismiss her tomorrow."

He grinned down at me and tapped the cast on my arm. "You can take this home to California as a souvenir."

"When can I get it off?" Already my arm felt hot and itchy.

"Six weeks, if you're a good girl and don't give your grandmother any more trouble." He scribbled something on the clipboard at the foot of the bed and walked out.

Gran pulled up a green plastic chair and sat down at the head of my bed. "You scared the devil out of me."

"That's good then," I said. "You're sure to go to heaven when you die."

Her eyes filled. "Please. Don't even say that word. I saw you lying there in the street and my heart stopped. If anything had happened to you . . ."

I felt awful. I had caused her nothing but

grief all summer long. First with that stupid episode with B.J. and my one pierced ear, then by driving the Mustang and scaring her half to death, and now this.

"I'm so sorry, Gran," I said. "I've been a royal pain all summer. I wouldn't blame you if you never wanted me to come here again."

"Don't be silly. You're my only granddaughter, and I love you more than anything." She squeezed my hand so hard it hurt, but it felt good at the same time.

We heard a muffled pop and whine and then the first of the Musslemans' fireworks exploded in the distance. Gran switched off the bright lights in my room and cranked my bed up so that I could see them without lifting my head. I scooted over to the edge of the bed and Gran climbed in beside me, holding me the way she used to when I was little. We watched the reds and greens, purples and blues bursting into flowers and stars, turning to showers of gold before burning out in the blue-black sky.

After a long time, I said, "Did you call Mom?"

"I tried." Gran sounded tired. "I don't know where she is." She shifted on the bed. "Your mother should get one of those answering machines. I feel stupid talking to a tape recorder, but they sure are handy sometimes."

"Gran?"

"Hmm?"

"How old is Eb?"

She raised herself up on one elbow. "What a strange question. Why do you ask?"

"Just curious."

I could feel her smile in the darkness. "So I noticed. You were staring a hole through the poor man at the breakfast table this morning."

"I didn't mean to. He just looked so different somehow. When I was little, I thought he must be nearly as old as Mom. But today he seemed a lot younger."

Gran chuckled. "He's considerably younger than your mother." She thought for a moment, then went on. "Let's see. Your Granddaddy's been gone five years now . . . that would make Eb twenty-two. Twenty-three come November."

"He's really nice, Gran. He made up a story about my needing glasses so I wouldn't be too embarrassed when he drove the—"

"Shh. Look."

Outside my window, dozens of sparklers and rockets exploded into a rainbow of colors. Then the United States flag shimmered against the sky.

"Isn't that something?" Gran murmured against my ear. "Makes a person want to stand up and salute."

"I don't think I could stand up if I had to."

"You need some sleep, darling. And so do I." She slid off the bed, smoothed her clothes and switched on the bedside light. "Would you like me to stay with you tonight? I can probably find a cot somewhere."

Deep down, I wanted her to stay. But even in the dim light, she looked so tired, so fragile, that I couldn't bring myself to ask. Especially since this whole thing was my fault—as usual. So I said, "Go on home, Gran. You'll sleep better in your own bed."

She straightened my bedcovers and handed me the call button. "You're not afraid?"

"I'll be okay." I managed a weak grin.

"All right, then. If you're sure."

"I'm sure. Go. Shoo. You're keeping me awake."

"You must be feeling better. You're getting sassy again."

I laughed. "I love you, Gran."

"Love you, toodles. See you in the morning."

The door swished shut. I tossed and turned, trying to get comfortable in the high, narrow bed. I would have been better off at home, too. Hospitals are noisy places. Out in the hallway, phones jangled, shoes squeaked on the tile floor, metal carts rattled along the corridors.

Finally I drifted off. I dreamed about Mom and the ranch and B.J. and Trey. And I dreamed about a strong, quiet ranch hand with dark, dancing eyes and a heart of pure gold. I dreamed of riding with him over our ranch land, with a child of our own in the saddle, and big noisy parties with a hundred guests all laughing together under the wide summer sky. I dreamed of lying next to him in the double bed at the ranch house, lulled by the river sounds and the steady beating of our own two hearts.

The door opened and B.J. rushed in, a blond tornado in sneakers. She threw herself across the bed, sending my breakfast tray clattering to the floor.

"My gosh, Jill! I can't believe it! Nearly killed by a fire truck! The most exciting things always happen to you."

She drew back and looked at me with an odd mixture of concern and fascination. "How did it happen? Tell me everything."

"I was crossing the street during the parade. I didn't see him coming."

"That's it? That's not much of a report from

a future news hound. Why were you crossing the street? What did it feel like when you got hit? Was the doctor who sewed you up cute?"

I rolled my eyes. "One. I was crossing the street to get to the other side."

"Old chicken joke," B.J. said. "Last time I heard that one I laughed so hard I fell into a pile of dinosaur bones."

I ignored that. "Two. I don't remember getting hit. I was crossing the street and I woke up here. And three, there was nothing to sew up. I got a bruised forehead and a broken arm. Nothing glamorous."

"And you broke your left arm at that! Too bad it wasn't your right. Think of all the chores you could have ducked. Was he cute?"

"Who?"

"The doctor, silly!"

"I don't know. I didn't pay much attention."

B.J. rolled her eyes. "I should have known. You're still such a tomboy. Not the least bit interested in men, are you?"

Something in her tone irritated me. I sat up in the bed. "You'd be surprised."

She took a compact out of her purse and studied her reflection in the mirror. She ran her little finger over her bottom lip, then snapped the compact shut. "So. Surprise me. Who do you like?"

Last night's dream flooded my senses and I shivered beneath the hospital blanket. "Well, he's older. Somebody I've known a long time."

"How much older?"

"A few years. But age isn't important. Even Mom says so."

"Do I know him?"

"Uh-huh."

"Well, who *is* it, Jill?" Suddenly her blue eyes narrowed. "Is it Trey?"

"Trey's super," I said, "but it's not Trey. Besides, I only met him a few weeks ago."

She grinned, mostly from relief, I thought. "Well, great! Maybe we can double-date before you go home. That is, if Trey will ever ask me out. Men! Sometimes, they're dense as fence posts."

"I thought he already *had* asked you out.

What about the time you went to the Dairy Queen with his cousin?"

"Oh that." She waved her hand dismissively. "That wasn't a real date. And besides, it was Ricky's idea, not Trey's."

"Oh."

"Anyway, who is it, Jill? The suspense is killing me! Who do you like?"

"Promise you won't tell?"

"Cross my heart and hope to die." She made an X in the air in front of her.

"Okay then. Here goes. It's Eb."

"Eb? Your grandmother's ranch hand? Lord, he's *ancient!*"

"He's twenty-two," I said. "That's not old."

"Jill, that's ten years' difference. He was already pitching in Little League the day you were born!"

"So? Granddaddy was eleven years older than Gran." I searched my mind for other examples. "And what about Scarlett O'Hara and Rhett Butler?"

"He left her in the end, Jill. Don't you remember? 'Frankly, my dear, I don't give a damn.' "

"Okay, so they're a bad example. They're just characters in a novel, anyway."

B.J. perched on the edge of my bed. "It won't work in real life, either. You have nothing in common. Does he know you like him?"

"Of course not! I would just die if he did."

"Then you'd better get that goofy look off your face every time you say his name or you'll give yourself away."

I shifted beneath the hospital blanket. "Don't worry. I hardly ever see him. Besides, I'll be going home after Gran's party."

"Speaking of parties," B.J. said, "I'm sorry you missed mine. It was the best one ever."

"Thanks a lot!"

She grinned and punched my good arm. "Sorry. Actually, it wasn't the best one ever." Her voice softened. "It wasn't the same without you. I missed you, Jill."

My eyes misted. For a moment, it seemed we'd gone back to a simpler time, to the way things were before this complicated summer. I squeezed her hand. "I missed you, too. What all did you get?"

"Let's see. The new skates, of course. But I'm only allowed to use them on the driveway. More earrings from Mom, and a couple of tapes. Grandma sent books—as usual."

"Anything good?"

"Naw." B.J. wrinkled her nose. "Baby stuff. I gave it all to my cousin, but don't you dare tell my mother."

"I won't. What else?"

She chewed on her lower lip for a minute. "Trey gave me a really neat poster."

"Oh yeah?" I tried to sound casual, but I was surprised at how jealous I felt. After all, I was in love with Eb. Why should I care if Trey gave her the whole moon? What was the matter with me? I felt totally mixed up.

"Yeah. It's a picture of the Milky Way. Did you know Earth is part of the Milky Way?"

"B.J., any third-grader knows that."

"Well, *I* didn't." She sounded hurt. "There's

more to life than being a bookworm. While you were holed up memorizing the encyclopedia, I was out having fun. You should get out more, Jill."

I stared out the hospital window at the mass of green treetops in the distance. "I guess."

She frowned. "What's the matter with you?"

Sudden tears rolled down my cheeks and I wiped them away. "I don't know. Maybe I'm losing my mind."

I gripped her hand with my good one. "Listen, Beej. Do you ever feel all mixed up inside, like your heart is . . . I don't know . . . too small to hold everything you're feeling?"

"Well, I—"

"Time's up!" A nurse poked her head in the door and motioned to B.J.

"Just a minute," B.J. said. "This is really important."

"Out. You're under age, young lady. You're not even supposed to be here without your parents."

B.J. shot me a helpless look.

"It's okay. I feel better now."

"You're sure? You want me to call your Gran?"

"Nah. She'll be here soon to take me home."

B.J. bent down to hug me. "I'll come over later then, okay?"

She picked up her purse and went out. The nurse took my temperature and read my chart. "Practically good as new," she said. "You were one lucky kid."

"I know."

She fluffed my pillows and filled the water pitcher. "Soon as Dr. McReynolds makes his morning rounds, we'll get you out of here. In the meantime, if you need anything, just press the call button."

"Okay."

When she left, I rolled out of bed and went to the mirror. What a royal mess. My ponytail hung in a dark tangle. Beneath the harsh glow of the blue hospital lights, my face looked pinched and pale. My arms and legs stuck out of the hospital gown like sticks. I brushed my hair and splashed water on my face and climbed back into bed to wait for Gran and Dr. McReynolds. I couldn't wait to get out of there.

The door swung open and in walked Eb.

My heart stopped. My mouth worked, but words wouldn't come out. I stared at him.

"Well, now," he said, stepping into the room. "Aren't you a sight for sore eyes? How're you feeling this morning, Miss Jill?"

"Better," I squeaked. I couldn't take my eyes off him. Eb in the flesh was even more spectacular than in my dream. Wonderful, I thought. Wonderful, wonderful, wonderful.

"That's good news. Scared me half to death when I heard what happened." He stood beside my bed, turning a new gray Stetson around and around in his perfect, slender fingers. Just watching that simple movement made my insides warm.

I wet my lips. "It's not that serious, really. I just wasn't paying attention. When this cast comes off, I'll be good as new."

White teeth flashed in his tanned face and

he shook his head. "I declare, woman, this has been some summer for you, hasn't it?"

Woman. He called me woman! Surely that meant he thought of me as something more than just a klutzy, skinny kid. Had he been dreaming of me, too? Overcome with a liquid feeling I couldn't name, I felt my cheeks turn warm, and I pulled the hospital blanket around my shoulders.

Eb didn't seem to notice. "Your Gran's down in the lobby. In the gift shop." He winked. "I expect you're in for a wonderful surprise."

I couldn't imagine any surprise more wonderful than having him standing there making a fuss over me. Despite the heavy, itchy cast on my arm, I'd never felt happier in my whole life.

He glanced out the window. "Nice view."

I nodded. "Gran and I watched the fireworks from here last night. It was almost as good as being down on the river."

"No kidding." The corners of his eyes crinkled when he smiled. "I'm glad you're all right."

"Thanks, Eb. Thanks for coming to see me."

"You bet." He turned toward the door. "I'd better get a move on. Can't keep Karen waiting too long."

Wham. It was like being hit in the stomach with a fastball. There was no air to breathe. "Karen?"

Then he smiled in a way I'd never seen before, like he was all lit up from the inside. "Oh, that's right, you haven't met her, have you?"

Right there in my hospital room, he fished a picture out of his wallet and handed it to me. "She's a special ed teacher in San Antone. We're getting married in December."

I stared at the photograph. Blond hair, of course. Blue eyes. Perfect teeth. It was all I could do to keep from ripping it to shreds, all I could do not to cry.

"She's a great gal," he said, retrieving the picture as if it were the Mona Lisa. "Say, if you're coming to the ranch for Christmas vacation, we'd love to have you come to the wedding."

A hard knot pulsed painfully in my throat. "I think I'm going skiing with my mother."

"Oh. Well, then. Guess I'll see you back at the ranch, as they say." He chuckled at his own joke.

I nodded, wishing he would just go before I shattered into smithereens.

He left and Gran came in with a new T-shirt and a teddy bear that would take up the whole back seat of the Mustang. I barely noticed. How could I? I was desperately in love with a man who was about to marry another woman!

Chapter Twelve

The night of Gran's party finally came. A pale moon nestled in the treetops. Fireflies flickered in the darkness like tiny versions of the Japanese lanterns that hung from our front porch, and the air smelled of honeysuckle and Gran's lemon-scented candles.

Gran wore her new pink dress and her pearls. I wore my blue dress and my cast. I stood just outside the yellow circle of porch light, watching the party.

Everybody in town had turned out to help Gran celebrate. Reverend and Mrs. Carson came, and the Swearingens and the Vosses, and the Cranes, who owned the furniture store. Trey came with his parents. The only one missing was Eb. He was back in San Antonio, picking out sheets and towels and fondue pots with Karen. Sue Ellen Coates arrived with her boyfriend on the back of a Harley Davidson, gave Gran a present and a kiss and rode off again.

"Well!" Gran said, fingering the silver-papered package. "Well! Did you ever?"

B.J.'s mother shook her head, and the gold hoops in her ears shimmered in the candle-light. "Those things scare me to death! If my daughter ever sets foot on one, I'll ground her for the rest of her life!"

"Oh, Motherrr!" B.J. rolled her eyes and grinned at me. "Come on, Jill. Let's eat."

We filled our plates and sat at one of the picnic tables set up on the lawn. Toby Crane and his parents sat down beside us. Mrs. Crane smiled at us, then started lecturing Toby as if he were nine years old instead of almost thirteen.

"Watch what you're doing, now. Don't spill that lemonade."

Toby's cheeks bulged. "I won't."

"Don't talk with your mouth full," Mr. Crane added. "And sit up straight."

B.J. grinned at me over the top of her red plastic cup and mouthed, "Poor Toby."

"*Oww!*" A howl erupted at the other end of the table. We looked up.

Bruce Swearingen's plump little grandmother shot from her chair, clutching her ample rear end with one hand and Bruce's ear with the other. "You *shot* me, you little devil!"

Bruce's slingshot dangled from his fingers. "Sorry, Gramma, I was aiming at that hoot owl."

"I don't care what you were aiming at! You had no business shooting at anything. You could put someone's eye out with that thing."

"Well, for Pete's sake, I had to do something for fun! This is the most boring birthday party I've been to in my whole life. There aren't even any games to play."

"Hush! Do you want Mrs. Lawrence to hear you? You sit down right there and don't you dare move a muscle until I tell you to. Do you hear me?"

"What's going on, Mama?" Bruce's mother shifted his baby sister to her other hip.

"This little criminal hit me with a slingshot," his grandmother said, licking barbecue sauce off her fingers. "I swear, Lula, you'll be lucky to keep him out of reform school till he turns eighteen."

Mrs. Swearingen held out her hand for Bruce's slingshot. "You're grounded for the rest of your life."

Bruce shrugged and gulped his lemonade. He'd been in enough trouble before to know she didn't really mean it.

"Hey, Jill," Toby Crane said. "I heard a secret about you."

I swung around. "What secret?"

He grinned. "Wouldn't you like to know?"

"Yes, I would. That's why I asked you."

"I'll give you a hint. It's about a b-o-y." He shot B.J. a knowing look. "Or should I say, a m-a-n. An *older* m-a-n."

My stomach lurched. I stared at B.J. "You told!"

I jumped up and ran past the tables laden with food, past the pink-draped bridge table holding Gran's chocolate birthday cake and its sea of flickering candles, down along the river and into the dark woods.

"Jill, wait!"

B.J.'s voice followed me into the night, but she was the last person I wanted to see. I hated her with a red, blinding rage unlike anything I'd ever felt before. How could she betray me, and to a stupid little shrimp like Toby Crane? I never wanted to see her again as long as I lived.

I curled up on the mossy riverbank and cried until I felt empty of everything. I cried because of my lost friendship with B.J., because everything had changed when I wanted it all to stay the same, because I loved Eb and he was going to marry Karen.

Behind me, the leaves rustled and I sat up and wiped my cheeks. "Go away, *Belinda*. I never want to speak to you again."

Trey chuckled. "That's the second time this summer you've mistaken me for B.J. Do we look that much alike?"

I smiled despite my black mood. "I thought she followed me down here."

He dropped onto the thick carpet of moss beside me and wrapped his arms around his knees. "You two fighting again?"

I shrugged. "I hate her."

"What's she done now?"

I didn't mean to tell him about my stupid, hopeless crush on Eb. But sitting beneath the dark canopy of trees, with music from Gran's party drifting over the water, it seemed that Trey and I were the only two people in the whole world. So I told him how I'd suddenly discovered Eb and how I'd dreamed about him while I was in the hospital, and how I'd told B.J. everything in strictest confidence, only to have her tell everything to that blabbermouth Toby Crane.

"I couldn't wait to get here for the summer," I finished. "I thought everything would be so perfect, and instead it's been the biggest disaster of my entire life."

Trey sat quietly for a long time, his arm barely touching mine. Finally he said, "Jill, haven't you figured out by now that things don't always turn out the way we want them to? Growing up is hard for everybody. Nobody has a perfect life."

"Except you."

"Me? I have the most messed up life of anybody."

I stared up at him in the darkness. "What's wrong with your life? You have a great dad, a beautiful mom—"

"Julie's my stepmom. My real mother lives in New Orleans. Or at least, that's where she was the last I heard." His voice sounded choked, as if he might cry.

"I didn't know that," I said. "You never said anything about it before."

"What's the point? Talking about it won't change anything."

He dug a rock out of the damp earth and

hurled it into the river. It sank with a loud
thunk, and the frogs went silent. Distant laughter drifted across the water.

I said, "My father lives in Japan, but I see
him when he comes back here on business.
Don't you ever see your real mom?"

"Nah. She's pretty busy, I guess. She moves
around a lot, so she said it would be best if I
lived with Dad and Julie."

I thought about the friendly, smiling woman
I'd seen around Trey's place all summer. "Julie
seems really nice, though."

"She's okay. She brings me stuff when
she and Dad go away on trips. But that'll probably change, too, once the new baby is
born."

He said it matter-of-fact, as if he'd been
thinking about it for a long time.

My mouth dropped open. "She's having a
baby? I don't believe you. She's not even fat or
anything."

"They just found out last week. Dad told me
yesterday. It won't be born till next March."

"Oh."

We listened to the crickets for a while. I said, "But don't you think it'll be neat to have a new brother or sister?"

"Neat? I think it's totally disgusting! The idea of people their age . . ."

For some reason, I started to giggle. I couldn't help it. Pretty soon Trey joined in, and we fell back on the moss and laughed till our sides hurt.

Finally Trey sat up, his face just inches from mine.

That's when it happened. That scary, exciting Ping-Pong feeling started up inside me again. We faced each other in the darkness. To me, it seemed as if the whole world had stopped turning, waiting for what was about to happen. I felt excited and confused and scared, all at the same time.

"Well," Trey murmured, "at least you don't seem so sad anymore."

"You either."

Then he leaned over and kissed me. His

mouth felt warm and strange. Above us, the stars whirled, caught, whirled again.

"You're a great girl, Jill," he said. Then he disappeared as quickly as he had come.

When I finally got up the next morning, I found Gran drinking coffee in the kitchen. I poured orange juice and rummaged in the cupboard for the corn flakes.

"Fighting with B.J. again?" She folded her newspaper and sipped her coffee.

"I hate her," I said simply. I opened the refrigerator, took out milk, then sliced a banana into my cereal bowl.

"That's a pretty strong statement."

"I mean it," I said. "If you can't trust your so-called best friend to keep your most secret secrets, then you might as well forget it." I dug my spoon into my cereal. "I hope I never lay eyes on B.J. Reynolds as long as I live."

"Oops," Gran said.

I looked up.

B.J. stood at the screen door, looking mournful as a lost puppy.

"Get off my porch!" I yelled.

"Come on in," Gran said.

B.J. came in and slid into the chair across from mine. I picked up my bowl and dumped my cereal into the sink and left the kitchen.

Five seconds later, Gran knocked on the door to my room and came in without waiting for an answer. She perched on the edge of my rumpled bed and fixed me with her dark, steady gaze.

"B.J. wants to talk to you."

"Well, I don't want to talk to *her*. Next time I want my private life broadcast, I'll call the TV station."

"You're hurt, sweetie. I know how you feel. But a friendship is a precious thing. You can't just throw it away like a worn-out sweater."

I rolled away from her and shut my eyes, trying not to listen. The last thing I wanted was a sermon on friendship.

But Gran kept talking. "Remember the day

we went down to the old pond, how overgrown it was? If we hadn't tended to it, it would have disappeared forever. We decided it was worth the effort to save it."

When I didn't move or speak, she went on. "You've been best friends with B.J. all your life. Don't you think you at least owe her a chance to explain? Just in case you still have something worth saving?"

I opened one eye. My new teddy bear stared at me with accusing amber eyes. "Oh, all right," I said. "If nothing else will do."

"Good girl. I'll send her right in." Gran patted my shoulder and hurried down the hall. Next thing I knew, B.J. appeared in the doorway.

"Well, don't just stand there like a stupid statue. Gran practically ordered me to talk to you." I stretched out on the bed and closed my eyes again. "What do you want?"

I heard her cross the room. "For starters, how about looking at me?"

I sat up and stared into her sapphire-blue

eyes. My anger shimmered in the room like a live thing. "Okay, I'm looking."

She winced, and her words tumbled out one on top of the other, like water over river rocks. "I'm sorry I told Toby Crane about you and Eb. It was a dumb thing to do and I don't blame you for being mad."

"You're right. It *was* dumb. And I'll never tell you another single thing as long as I live."

I guess that was the wrong thing to say, because her face got red and she let me have it with both barrels. "I couldn't care less what you tell me, Jill, and if you're going to be so snotty, I'm sorry I even bothered to apologize."

"Well, then, why didn't you just stay home where you belong?"

"My mother *made* me come over here, if you want to know the truth. I told her you'd be hateful about it."

"Well, what did you expect, B.J.? Toby's got a mouth bigger than Dallas. By now half of Texas knows how I feel about Eb. Do you realize I'll never be able to show my face in town again? I can't believe you did this to me!"

"I didn't mean to, Jill. We were goofing around and it just slipped out. Anyway, I said I was sorry! What else can I do?" B.J. stood with her hands on her hips, waiting for an answer.

"From now on, just keep your nose out of my business."

"Fine! Then stay out of mine! And stay away from my friends!"

"What are you talking about?"

"As if you don't know! Trey was *my* friend, and now all he talks about is you. 'Jill this,' 'Jill that.' I'm sick of it!"

"Well, don't worry. I'm going home soon and you'll have him all to yourself."

"I don't *want* him!" B.J. stamped her foot. "Who wants to go around with some stupid boy who's always talking about some other girl?"

"I can't help it if he likes me."

"Oh, listen to you. Little Miss Innocent. As if you haven't bent yourself out of shape all summer long trying to impress him."

"I don't know what you're talking about!"

"Oh no?" Her voice went up an octave. 'Look, Trey, Galileo!' And what about driving the car to the Steakout that time? By the way, I know Eb was lying about your glasses. You've never worn glasses in your whole life. Is that why you fell in love with him, Jill? Because he lied for you?"

"Shut up!" I said. "Just get out of my room and out of my house."

"This isn't your house. It's your Gran's." She didn't budge.

"Well, it will be someday. It's in Gran's will. So there!"

"Big hairy deal. That's about as big a deal as your wearing a bra to the Fourth of July parade." Her eyes narrowed. "Bruce Swearingen told me all about it. Which you didn't need, by the way. Prob'ly won't need one for ten years at least. Maybe you'll *never* grow boobs, Jill.

Maybe you'll be flat as a board till the day you die."

"Shut *up*, Belinda!" My throat closed up and I fought back tears.

"Shut up yourself."

"I hate you!"

"Ooooh, as if I even care!" B.J. stood with one hand on the doorknob. "I hate you, too, and I hope you never come back here again."

"Oh, I'll be back to see Gran, but don't worry. I certainly won't bother *you*."

"Good!" B.J. ran down the hall, through the kitchen and out the door. Her footsteps pounded along the wooden porch.

I yanked open the window and stuck my head out. "Fine! That's just fine with me!"

Then I threw myself on the bed and cried so hard I thought my heart would actually break into a million pieces. B.J. and I had had fights before, but nothing like this.

Gran came in and I told her everything. About Eb and Karen, about Trey kissing me in the dark down by the river, and about B.J. never wanting me to come back to Texas.

"She doesn't mean it," Gran soothed. "She's just scared is all."

"Scared? Of what?"

"Of losing you. And Trey. She feels left out. You have spent a lot of time with him this summer. And now you're angry with her."

"She started it! She started everything. This whole summer she's acted like she's this really smart adult, and I'm still just a dumb kid. Every time Trey came around she tried to make me look stupid."

Gran plucked at a loose thread on the quilt. "Sometimes I think I'd give a million dollars to be young again, then something like this happens to remind me of how painful it all was. It's a miracle we survive it." She held out her hand and helped me to my feet. "Come on. You never finished your breakfast."

The thought of food made me gag, but I followed her out to the kitchen, to our places at the table. Sunlight poured into the room and glinted off the aluminum coffeepot on the counter. From his perch in the pecan tree, a lone mockingbird scolded and fluttered. Gran sipped her coffee and rubbed at an imaginary spot on the red-and-white checked tablecloth. Finally she said, "Remember Cissy Evans? You saw her at my birthday party."

"The one with red hair and the rhinestone glasses?"

Gran grinned. "Aren't they awful? Yes, that was Cis, all right. We've been friends for fifty years. Dated the same boy in high school."

I stared at my grandmother. It was hard to imagine her as a young girl, going out with boys. I'd always imagined her with Granddad. Nobody else.

"Oh, I know what you're thinking!" Gran chuckled. "Believe it or not, I cut quite a figure in my day. Could have married anyone I wanted."

"But you only wanted Granddad, right?"

"Of course. But that came much later. Back in high school Buddy Shelton was the one everybody wanted. That black-haired rascal was going steady with Cis and me at the same time, only neither of us knew it. Until the night

I saw the two of them coming out of the Texas Twin Theater. I was furious. Didn't speak to Cis for a whole week."

She looked at me, hard. "That week without my best friend seemed about a year long. It was the worst week of my life."

"How did you get her back?"

"Wrote her a note. Left it in her locker right after lunch. Told her exactly how I felt about everything."

"Did she write you back?"

Gran shook her head. "After supper that night, I was sitting on the back steps with Mama, snapping beans, when here comes Cis, driving her daddy's old Ford pickup. I remember, she was so short she could barely see over the steering wheel. 'That fool girl's gonna kill herself,' my daddy said, but of course she didn't."

She sipped her coffee and smiled wistfully. "We talked and yelled and said terrible things to each other, and then we cried and talked some more. Cis ended up staying all night at my house. We decided our friendship was more important than Buddy Shelton, that two-timing devil!"

The story was so interesting that I forgot for a moment about my fight with B.J. "What happened to him?"

"Married a girl from Harlingen and had seven kids, last I heard. All boys. But that's not important. The point is, a good friend can get you through a lot in life. I don't know what I would have done without Cis when your granddaddy died."

Then I remembered every detail of the day Granddad went to the hospital. The ambulance that came all the way from Austin; Mom and Gran and Aunt Gina, their faces pale and tear-stained; and a stocky, red-haired woman who moved quietly through the ranch house taking care of food and flowers and calming one scared seven year old. Me.

"She let me make peanut butter cookies," I said.

"You needed to do something normal that

day. Cis knew that. She's been here for every good thing and every bad thing that's ever happened to me."

Gran let out a little sigh. "Oh, we've had our ups and downs over the years, but I love her like a sister, and I never take her for granted."

I got the message. I'm not stupid. But right then I didn't see how I could ever ask B.J. to come back. Not after what she'd done. It wasn't until later, after I'd imagined being back in L.A. without her letters to look forward to, after I'd thought about next summer at Gran's without her, that I swallowed my pride and wrote her a note. I mailed it right away, before I had a chance to get mad all over again and change my mind.

Chapter Thirteen

"Hey, Jill, it's me." B.J. peered at me through the screen door of the sleeping porch. "Can I come in?"

"Okay."

I tried to sound casual, but my heart beat like a trip-hammer. It had been three whole days since I'd sent the letter, and I'd begun to think I never would see B.J. again. She came in, letting the screen door slap shut behind her, keeping one hand on the door handle, as if she might have to leave in a hurry.

We looked at each other for what seemed like forever. Finally she said, "I got your letter."

"It's about time. I thought the post office had lost it."

"Naw. I went to Dallas with Mom." She

glanced around. "Where's your grandmother?"

"Out helping Eb. Puddin cut her leg on the fence. They've called the vet."

"Your Gran sure is crazy about that calf. Will Puddin be okay?"

We circled the real reason for B.J.'s visit like two boxers circling the ring, but I was too scared to just up and ask her if we were ever going to be friends again. So I kept talking about Gran and the calf, but I was thinking about happier times with B.J.—the winter we got six inches of snow and school closed for three days, and B.J. and I made snowmen in our meadow; the time I forgot my math homework and B.J. gave me hers; the day in second grade when I beat up on Bruce Swearingen because he called B.J. a towhead and made her cry; the night at summer camp when we stole bubble gum from the concession stand and then stayed awake till dawn, praying for God not to strike us dead.

"Hey," B.J. said softly. "What's the matter with you?"

I stared past her shoulder at the shaft of sunlight slanting across the floor. "Nothing."

"You're crying."

"I am not."

"Are too."

"Am not."

But I was. We both were.

"I'm sorry, Jill," B.J. blubbered. "I didn't mean all those awful things I said."

With my good arm, I hugged her. I was bawling, too, but it was one of the happiest moments of my life. "Me either," I said. "I don't hate you. I never could."

She pulled away from me, grinning through her tears. "And I take back what I said about your figure. Actually, I think you look great. I'm jealous."

But she didn't mean that either. B.J. has always been prettier than me, and she knows it. It's a point in her favor that she never makes a big deal out of it.

Just then, Gran came up the steps and into the kitchen. When she saw the two of us standing on the porch, bawling like two motherless calves, she turned around and went out again.

My last morning at the ranch. I slip out of bed while the house still sleeps and head for the river, down past the cattle standing patiently in the wet grass, past the barn and the tool shed and the neat rows of peach trees along the road.

A silver mist hangs above the water. The sleeping birds make dark shapes in the trees. I climb onto our elm and scoot out to the edge, scraping my back on the rough bark. Beneath my bare legs, the ridged branches feel damp and solid. Above me, the stars wink out and I wonder if Trey is watching them too, still looking for answers in the sky.

It's funny, but I already miss him. And Gran. Most of all, I miss B.J. We've changed this summer, more than I ever thought we could. More than I ever wanted. But this much I know; we'll always be best friends, no matter what.

It says so, right here on my bracelet.